About the Author

Aimee has grown up on a farm in Sussex and spent most of her life outside or creating in some form or another. She currently resides in Wiltshire where she continues her writing.

Do I Know You?

Aimee Silver

Do I Know You?

Olympia Publishers
London

www.olympiapublishers.com
OLYMPIA PAPERBACK EDITION

A CIP catalogue record for this title is
available from the British Library.

ISBN: 978-1-78830-580-8

First Published in 2022

Olympia Publishers
Tallis House
2 Tallis Street
London
EC4Y 0AB

Printed in Great Britain

Dedication

For Granny. I will always love you.

Chapter One

Sunlight bounced down in small lines through the white wooden blind. I tried to force one eye open. It was still sticky from the night before. Creases of mascara glued themselves to my tear duct. Feeling a slight comedown fast approaching, I reached for the cord and managed to grab it with little effort. Sunlight would cease the feelings of doubt and assist in me completely forgetting the night before. I could relive it another time when my sinuses weren't threatening to set light to my face.

The hot shower woke me slightly but the dull ache of depression and loneliness would not wash away with my fruity shampoo. It was the same cycle of regret and making myself numb. I had to break it, break free from cocaine. Life was surely worth more than this? A life led by heavy emotions and inability to deal with them was not a successful one.

"Why don't you try speed instead?" Alex was helping me stack the baked bean shelf at our place of religion. I say religion, I mean work but the amount of time I spent here, it felt like it should be something I was into, like religion.

Ugh.

Society was full of all these things I should or shouldn't be doing. I thought I was a free spirited individual but the amount of times I had become obsessed with a fad or something equally as brainless, I had to question why I had imagined I was any different in the first place.

"I've not particularly enjoyed my previous speed sessions." I cocked my head to the side and watched Alex stack the bean tins one by one. His face was screwed up with concentration and his tongue was poking out the side of his moustache tickled mouth. Bean tin stacking was quite a feat for my lovely but slow friend.

"I dropped a bomb in the bogs earlier, it helps me stack faster man."

"You serious?"

"Yup. Usually I save it as my Saturday morning thing at work but Wednesdays are just dragging so bad I'd thought I jump start my hump day." He nodded his head so much that his curly black hair bounced onto his forehead. He had afro hair and muddy brown eyes. At a tall 5ft 7 he towered above most midgets and had tiny feet. I never wanted to know if the foot/penis thing was actually a thing with him and so, sorry, I can't divulge that information.

This news didn't shock me in the slightest even though I will admit I had no clue he was dropping at work. I wasn't entirely convinced it did any good, considering the length of time it took him to put a customer through the tills.

I crouched down to focus on the lower shelf. I liked

Alex; he was easy to be around and he didn't try and hit on me. Well, at least if he had I had never noticed. He was like a brother I never had and even though I would never tell him, I was real glad he was here.

I could feel my nose running slightly but not enough to warrant a tissue so I opted for a sneaky sleeve wipe. Lucky I did as an ugly blood stain formed on my cuff. I uttered a few excuses to Alex before skidding down the aisle to the staff toilets.

The strip lights in the cramped toilets were less than friendly on any normal day. Today they were particularly nasty to my pale complexion, highlighting the dark circles radiating beneath my eyes. I gazed into my grey blue eyes and wondered how I had got to this point. My reflection wanted to lecture me about drugs. I turned away and pulled some bog roll off to shove up my nose like a tampon. I quickly ruffled my long, dark chestnut hair and straightened my scratchy red polo top. I loved my work uniform. Not.

"You alright, man? You left pretty quickly and I was going to offer to give you a bump, thought it might perk you up."

"Thanks, Alex, but I will pass on that one. I'm going to move over to the tills and hopefully it will make the shift finish faster."

"Fair enough bro, hit me up at lunch yeah?"

"Sure. Catch you later." I followed the too short aisle up to the tills and perched myself on a grubby blue swivel chair. I pushed the levers to get the right height and signed myself in on the plastic covered touchpad till. I wondered if there was more than this out there, more than a cycle of getting through the work day and coping with snorting each night to numb the deadness inside. A brief and fleeting flicker of hope fluttered past before I made the decision, forty-five minutes into my shift, that dinner would be forgone and my dealer met instead.

I used to think I was cool, having cocaine for dinner. Now I just realised what a mess I was and how I had to keep going to forget about it.

I want to say the rest of the day passed in a breeze but we all know I would be lying. Anyone who has ever worked in customer service knows that your day stretches and bends in time like Dali's melting clocks.

It was cold on the corner of Bright Flower Street. My burgundy scarf had unravelled itself and was now trailing down my back. I stopped to fight with it and was winded by someone walking straight into me. Their hands held my waist like a lover as they steadied themselves and initial panic set in and started to burn in my chest.

I hated being touched at the best of times, especially this, now – with a stranger. I scrambled for their hands at my waist. Trying to step back and, nuzzling into the comfort of my scarf, I was able to look up and size up who I might be up against.

The streetlamp didn't work on this exact corner nor did the ones across the road. That's mainly why I met my dealer here. I strained my eyes to look for notable details about this person and even though I ate my carrots, I was having difficulty seeing this evening.

They were at least a foot taller than Alex, with a long

winter jacket on. Looming eerily above me they let out a low growl of words.

"Watch where you're going sweetheart, you don't know what kind of trouble you might run into..."

I gasped and tried to step again back but his hands stayed strong on my waist.

"Sometimes it feels like danger and sometimes it feels like heaven." He leant closer to me and I could make out eyes the same colour as mine. Usually I don't like eye contact but I relaxed into his firm grip. It was like my body had a mind of its own and it wanted to be closer to him.

I could smell faint wood smoke and a hint of cologne. He smelt like the sea and the sun and I risked another peek into his eyes. Again my body sagged in relief, it made my head spin...

"Anna, I have been waiting for you." He whispered and a glint of white showed his smile in the faded light.

"How do you... How do you know my name?" I stammered.

"Do you know why you take drugs? Do you know why you consistently numb your abilities?"

"What? How do you know? Who are you?" I shook my head in disbelief.

"Maybe the same way that you know things but you're just too full of shit to recognise how special you are! I had hoped you would figure it out on your own but you just don't get it!"

"Special? I think you have the wrong person there man!" I was getting it now; he was probably just some druggy waiting for the same guy as me. That must be how he knew I took drugs and maybe he was having some kind of crisis and he wanted to project it on to me. Yep, rationality and realism saves the day again.

"Your heart is disagreeing with the formula you've just concocted to decipher who I am and what I'm talking about. I guess I will have to try a little harder to get into those sky high walls of yours." He released me and slipped one of his hands into mine. He threw one last smirk at me before guiding us along the uneven pavement.

Who the hell was he? I snuck glances at him as the street light washed over his features. His long blonde hair moved slowly as he walked with ease. He had a neatly kept beard and a nose ring. Man he was hot. Suddenly my palm became particularly sweaty in his as I panicked at how good looking he was.

I was treated to another smirk as his lip curled upward and I then felt indignant.

"Listen, you!" I stopped walking and he turned to face me. "Just because you're all hot and stuff does not mean you can take me off somewhere and just smirk at me like I'm some kind of thing!" I wanted to stomp my foot for extra effect but I kept it inside. His eyes levelled, how was it possible that they were just like mine? They crinkled at the sides as he started to laugh and much to my annoyance it was a beautiful laugh that made me want to join in.

"Stop being a dick and don't ever do drugs again." His eyes flashed and his mouth became a flat line after he spoke. I scowled back at him and followed him as he set of down the road again.

Why was I going with him? Did I have no self-respect? What if he raped me? My brain went off on a sick fantasy tangent and I shook my head to rid myself of mental images, him sweaty and naked wasn't exactly going to make me run the other way.

His lip curled upwards again and I wondered if he could hear my thoughts or see inside my brain.

I focused on my surroundings and the moonlight shafting down through the fiery leaves. This was nuts, this was insane but inside I was massively enjoying it. Maybe he was right about listening to my heart.

"I'm always right." He winked and we turned down a red brick lane, lined with shiny black doors and golden doorknockers. It was obviously a competition on whose knocker was the best and one was almost as big as the door itself.

"Get out of my head!" I muttered as he pulled me down into a side path I hadn't noticed before. He stopped briefly to touch my face and look at my mouth. Why I was allowing this kind of behaviour I will never know but I couldn't pull away. My mouth responded with excitement as he leant in for a kiss but he just brushed past to whisper in my ear that he was gay and I had nothing to worry about.

My heart sank and I wanted to push him away in a childish sulk. I felt stupid for thinking anything would be going on in a romantic way. I mean just look at him!

Chapter Two

"Long time no see." Charlie cocked his trilby ever so slightly to the left. I picked at the scraps of dull aubergine nail varnish on my thumb whilst he paid for his meal deal. My stomach was churning between last night's line I craftily saved for this morning and an intense hunger since missing breakfast, lunch and dinner yesterday. I shook my head at the sandwich selection and grabbed a vitamin drink (the same price as Charlie's whole meal deal) and jumped the queue beside him.

The old lady in front kept up a display of lip pursing and looks designed to kill. I did not have the capacity to care. It could have been the tattoos Charlie had covering most of his body apart from his face but I could feel the daggers flying in my direction.

"Where you been then, babe?" His hand propelled me gently in front of him as the queue shuffled forwards. His touch lingered on the small of my back, whether or not his hand was still there, I did not know. I moved away but the feeling stayed. I realised I had never looked to see what colour eyes Charlie had. After last night and my mixed up dreams I must have been high – really high.

That man with my eyes and his odd abilities... I would have to get some more so I could lose myself in a fantasy world with him.

I looked across at Charlie and his short dark hair. He locked sight with me and relief spread through me as green glittered back.

"Are you okay, Anna? You look even worse than usual." A small smile tugged at the corner of his lips. I feigned hurt and pushed him out of the queue. The daggers from the old woman became more intense, it was almost painful. I turned away from her; I couldn't cope with facing her head on.

I wondered quietly whether it was too early to meet Pete, my dealer.

Charlie sat under a tree in Lizzie Gardens and tore chunks of chicken club sandwich with razor sharp teeth. I sipped on my vitamin drink and sent a text to Pete.

"Is everything alright, mate?" Charlie asked through lumps of bread.

"Yeah, man, same old. What about you?"

"I'm okay, I've just been making this new long board and trying to incorporate a new type of resin..." His voice faded into the background as a stronger male one forced its way into my head.

"Why are you lying to him?"

I slowly looked around me so Charlie thought I was still listening to him. That man wasn't anywhere to be seen and I was sure that he had been a hologram made up by my lonely and sad brain. Maybe I should go to the doctors, no matter how much I hated them. I had heard about this kind of behaviour before and once you left reality you ended up drooling in a white room, staring out the window, locked in a world of dreams.

"You are not mad, Anna."

The voice merged into my inherent thought pattern and I had to hide my panic from Charlie. He had leant his back against the safe cracks of the old oak tree and the autumn sun glowed high in the sky. I tried to focus on nature and the happiness it always gave to me. I felt the cold grass beneath my fingers and the warmth of the knowing sun. I imagined myself as a glass being filled with golden sunlight. I felt a hand on my shoulder and my eyes sprang open expecting to see Charlie's frowning face. Instead those eyes were there, he was there. I must be going mad, he wasn't real.

"Charlie, isn't it?" His eyes crinkled as he reached the hand that wasn't on my shoulder in Charlie direction.

"Yeah, man, sorry I don't think we've met before? What's your name?" Charlie gripped his hand and pumped it briefly.

"No we haven't met but I have heard a lot about you! My name is Xavier, I am a good friend of Anna's." He turned back to me before removing his hand and sitting cross legged next to me. He was wearing flowery board shorts, a black quicksilver hoody and flip flops. His long blonde hair was tied in a loose bun at the base of his neck. In the light of day he was even better looking and his eyes twinkled at me as I drank him in. I shot a look at Charlie to see if this was real and he could see Xavier too but he was checking him out and seeming impressed.

"Charlie, how is your girlfriend? I'm sorry I forgot to

ask!" I breezed in.

"Ah, she is fine. We've not seen that much of one another recently and she is thinking about going travelling to Thailand. I'm not sure how to take it to be honest!"

"Why don't you go with her?" I kept my focus on Charlie and his tilted hat but I could feel a full power smirk aimed at me from Xavier.

"What about you, Xavier? Do you have a partner?" Charlie looked over to him and completely ignored my suggestion.

"I prefer to be alone, it keeps my head clear and I know who I am without taking on the energy of other people."

"I hear you, man. That's why I am wondering whether Tammy going to Thailand is actually a blessing in disguise. I mean I do love her and she's hot..."

"But you can't connect with her? You can't talk to her properly? Same dreams and goals are important, dude!"

They continued to chat and I had to ensure my mouth wasn't hanging open in shock. As if it wasn't painful enough that Xavier was that good looking, everything he said was as if he was stringing out my thoughts from my clouded head. My stomach tied knots inside and I felt at a loss. I must be really sick if I thought he hadn't been real and even sicker if I could hear him inside my head.

Where had he come from? Had he been here all along?

I picked at my old, fraying Converse and checked to see if Pete had messaged back. I knew Charlie had to head back to work soon and Pete was ready to meet me in twenty minutes on our corner. I stood up and took my walls with me.

"You off now, mate? It was good to catch up with you again. Don't leave it so long next time okay? I do worry about you sometimes." Charlie stood up and hugged me before ruffling my hair.

"Good to see you, man." I mumbled before turning and heading across the park. I heard Xavier and Charlie exchanging goodbyes and the beat of running on the ground. The thumps from his feet got louder as he pulled my arm to a stop.

"Where are you going? Don't go and meet him again Anna. I let you off last night but you have to stop or it will kill you."

"You're not real. Go away."

"Wait. What? Not real? What on earth makes you think that?"

"You can't be real. I won't allow it." I sulked looking to the ground.

"Why is that, Anna? Is it because you might have to accept who you actually are and stop hiding from the world. It's easy to take drugs. It is easy to deny yourself what life is actually about." He looked deep into my eyes and I felt a tug in my stomach. He was looking into my soul and assessing me and I didn't like it. I did that to other people, no one did it to me.

I released my arm from his strong grip and turned to leave. The leaves swirled dangerously around me and the sun burned brighter. I felt anger hissing out of the palm of my hands and Xavier didn't move away. His screwed up face told me he could feel it but he stayed put. My blood felt like it was bubbling and boiling and I flashed my eyes at him.

"Let me in." He murmured quietly.

"No. I can't, it never works." My ears roared and I took a step back.

"I don't need saving, Xavier. I have to learn to save myself before I can let other people in."

"Who told you that? Who told you that you have to take the world on your shoulders? What if you let the right people in and they unblocked all that power and love that you've got bottled up in there. I can see it. You've done a good job and keeping it all locked away."

"One of the few things I'm good at." I muttered petulantly. He gently took my hand and my heart slowed. The pain in my chest eased and I shut my eyes; I was exhausted. I was tired of fighting, tired of running and tired of not loving. I let him pull me into his arms and I rested my head against his warmth. Silent tears rolled down my crumpled face as he caged me in safety. I hadn't been vulnerable since time began and it was a bittersweet release. The shadows from the trees danced slowly round as the fiery orb sank lower into the black. This was my favourite time of day but I usually spent it locked in my room doing drugs or under the fluorescent lights at work.

I missed nature and all the things that made me feel alive. I had been dying and speeding it up. I hadn't allowed myself to love or take on energy. I had built my walls up so high and my light was burning so low it resembled the end of a tea light, swimming in its waxy death. Time moved slowly but the inky twilight sky and sparkle of the first stars told me different. I hated to be touched, my brother Bill knew this all too well and found it hilarious to sit next to me with his hand on my back. I would flinch away from anyone and choose to stand back when talking.

Xavier stroked my hair as I snivelled into his jumper that was damp from my salty tears.

"Come on, let's get you in the warm." He kept an arm around me and guided me across the rest of the darkened park.

We turned along a street I didn't know and to a blue door that had a small brass letterbox. The paint was weathered and cracked and there was a little bit of moss growing on the wooden doorstep.

My anxious thoughts kept trying to force their way in but it was as if he had created shield around me, a shield just so I could be myself and be vulnerable.

He gestured for me to walk through the doorway first and as I did he flipped the light switch. The sea grass carpet was rough under my feet as I kicked off my Converse. The walls were painted cream and a soft, brown leather sofa dominated the floor space. Books lined one wall and a large, azure acrylic seascape another.

"I'm making food."

"I don't want any thanks."

"Yeah sure. Pasta it is."

I sank into the sofa whilst he moved into the kitchen. I checked my phone to see lots of missed calls from Pete. I text back to let him know I couldn't make it. I knew he would be screwing for the time I had left him waiting on that ominous corner. I felt guilt rising in my gut and

Xavier appeared with a glass of orange juice and lemonade.

"Thanks."

"You're more than welcome. If you want to put any music on then go ahead, I don't have a TV but I guessed that doesn't really bother you though." He smiled before heading back into the kitchen.

I gratefully took a long sip of my drink. All that crying had given me a headache of dehydration. I set my glass carefully on the oak side table before padding over to the music system. I decided on vinyl as I found his collection was impressive. Ben Howard's *Noonday Dream* album began its journey. I hadn't listened for so long. I had been denying myself music. Music made my soul sing, it made everything make sense. I could sing, I could play but I didn't. I locked all my talents up in a world of self doubt and stupidity. Some people would give their right arm for the talents I had but I refused to use them.

I moved back to the safety of the sofa and I could smell garlic and tomato wafting through from the kitchen. My stomach rumbled in protest and I hadn't realised how hungry I was. I closed my eyes and let Ben's soul and fire wash over me. His words cleansed my pent up ball of energy. It was as if each lyric let me know that he knew and it pulled a string from the ball and kept unravelling, the silvery strings creating a glowing web across the ceiling.

"Beautiful!" Xavier murmured and my eyes fluttered open. I was greeted with his smile and a steaming bowl of pasta. He hadn't been shy with the cheese, he knew how it should be.

We ate in companionable silence and I felt the warmth of the food spread throughout my cold and old body.

"It's good to see you glow." He took my empty plate from me and I went to stand up. "It's okay; I have a dishwasher and I do think you need some rest. I made sure this house had a bath because, well you know how amazing a bath is. The towels are clean in there and I'll grab you some of my clothes you can sleep in."

"Xavier…"

"Yes Anna?"

"Thank you."

I moved to the stairs and headed up. There were a few doors but I soon found the bathroom. The floor was large slate tiles and a massive roll top bath stood proudly at one end. The floor was deliciously heated and I wasted no time in running the bath and throwing some Himalayan bath salts into the running water. I stepped out of my tear and grief stained clothes and dipped into the warm water. The record player had been turned right up, so that I could hear another album being played. I loved Ludovico Einaudi and it was perfect as I sunk my head below the water to rinse the shampoo lather from my hair.

I stepped out of the bath and into one of the massive towels from the radiator. I noticed one of Xavier's t-shirts and a pair of his boxers folded up neatly by the door. How had I not noticed the door open? For the first time I was glad Xavier was gay so I didn't need to worry about him seeing me in the bath; not that I really wanted anyone to see me. I borrowed his hairbrush and hung my towel back up. His shirt hung a little loose over my curves and the boxers fit well. I always worried with previous boyfriends that I was too big for their clothes but I never was and never had been. I screwed my old clothes into a ball and tucked them in the top of his washing basket. I used his toothbrush, I didn't want to be waking up with a garlic mouth in the morning.

I stepped into the hallway and there was another door open and the room was bathed in a glow from the lamp beside the bed. The bed was massive and so comfy. It had been many months since I had gone to bed without being high and sleep came quickly.

I awoke with a start in the middle of the night and wondered where I was. The bedside light had been switched off and I could feel his warmth beside me. It was nice not having to worry that he might try and have sex with me; it gave me the ability to let my walls down a little. There was no anxiety or fear for his ulterior motives, even though the devil inside of me groaned in sexual frustration because he was so hot and kind. I knew it was right and exactly what I needed. My brain started to chatter away to itself and I felt his arm wrap around me and pull me close to him.

"Go back to sleep. It's okay," he mumbled and nestled his face into my hair.

Chapter Three

Sunlight was trying to creep in around the curtains and even though they did a pretty good job at blacking out the room, I was now able to see it properly. The carpet was a soft cream and the walls the colour of the sky in the height of summer. An old, long surfboard stood up against one wall and a couple of wetsuits, his clothes hung from the open rail. Xavier was fast asleep on the gunmetal grey bedding so I slid out of the bed gently and grabbed a black hoody off the railing. It was big and warm as I pulled it over my head and snuggled into it. The door was thankfully quiet as I tiptoed over to it and went to the bathroom.

This was the awkward part about staying at someone else's house, what do you do when you need to shit? I turned the big rain shower on and stuffed toilet roll down the loo, making sure that I locked the door this time. Xavier might be gay but I don't ever want to be walked in on when I'm mid clear out. After I washed my hands and tied my hair up, I thought I might as well have my morning shower whilst I was here.

The kitchen was tiled in the same slate as the

bathroom, with light grey walls. It was open plan with a white, wood island in the middle. Although I was hungry, I was more interested in what was beyond the huge window. Dinner plate headed peach Dahlias swung gently in the breeze and a terracotta path wound its way to the bottom of the garden. There was a sparkle of a mirror at the end wall and it looked like a gateway into another world. I felt a pull towards it and walked over to the French doors.

"You're not dressed for the cold." Xavier's hand covered mine on the door handle.

"But I want to see what it is."

"Not yet, you've only got boxer shorts on for a start and anyway, you can't go down there okay. Promise me that you won't go down there?"

"Okay..." I looked up into his pale eyes and he was serious. "What is down there?"

"Nothing you need to worry about. One day I will take you there." He removed my hand from the door and steered me to a seat at the kitchen island. I flinched as my hand touched the cold, white marble worktop. I studied him as he moved around the kitchen and started making breakfast. He put thin rashers of bacon into a pan and starting scrambling some eggs in a cup. The smell was amazing, I loved food but I had been neglecting myself for so long. My fat thoughts went to my little podge belly and I looked over at the food again with drool in my mouth.

"Before you say you can't eat because of some stupid idea you have of how you look, you will be eating and we can go for a run some when don't worry."

I blanched slightly but it was at how he knew me so well when I had only known him for a few days. I had wanted to go running for ages but I just never got round to it. The heavy smoking and torrent of drug abuse made me feel weak and tired all the time. I was intimidated because Xavier was clearly a lot fitter than I was but I loved running and I was weirdly good at it. I guess I needed to stop making excuses and suck it up.

Xavier pushed a plate of bacon and scrambled eggs on seeded brown bread towards me. It looked so good and the little pig inside of me seriously considered shoving my face into it. I choose my knife and fork like a normal human being before commencing shovelling it into my mouth.

"You need some stuff from your house don't you?" Xavier asked.

"Yeah just running stuff."

"I've been thinking that you should get your things and stay here for a while. I work quite a lot so you will have the house to yourself for most of the time. I know it seems an odd request but as a friend I can see that you're killing yourself. I have the facility to get you on track and get you out of this depression."

"You want me to move in?"

"Yeah and I want you to quit your job and find something better suited to you."

"But I don't have anything but debts and you don't want me registered at this address."

"I know you will sort it out but there will be no smoking or drugs and definitely no ex-boyfriends that treated you like shit."

"I don't know."

"Do you want to get better, Anna?"

"Yes."

"Then call your job and call your landlady." He smiled at me and I trusted him.

I had been naive before and I may well be that now but he made me feel safe and like my life might finally make sense again. He was right, I needed to sort it out and running from myself and my past hurts would not do me any good anymore. I finished my food and there was a flash in the reflection of the fridge door. I was almost certain it came from the bottom of the garden.

"I'll clean up here, go make those phone calls sweetheart." Xavier handed me my phone. I don't even remember where I'd left it. He propelled me into the sitting room before closing the kitchen door behind me. Huh. That was rude. Never mind. I had to make these calls and I wasn't sure which would be more daunting.

Chapter Four

My boss was a frizzy haired control freak who had hated
me since about three minutes into my first shift. I had
started with enthusiasm but it filtered out and was now
more of a case of when I could be bothered I would work
hard. Her name was Carol and she was a nasty,
manipulative bitch. She had never said that she didn't like
me but I could feel her invisible beef radiating from her.
Carol loved to hit me with her sickly sweet smile and best
friend bullshit but I knew. I knew she was a behind the
scenes backstabber and I hated making money for her. I
dialled her personal number and waited sourly as it rang.

"Hello, Anna!" Her voice trilled down the phone and
I could hear her talons clacking away on the keyboard.
Her fingers were like fat pigs in high heeled shoes.

"Hi, Carol. Look I'm really sorry for doing this over
the phone and I want to thank you for the opportunities
you have given me but I won't be able to work for you
anymore."

There was silence on the end of the phone and I
wondered whether there was steam coming out of her.

"Well I think that you should have let me know

before in person but as it happens I have hired someone else who can take your shifts on. I do believe you haven't taken your holiday either and so that will be added on to your final pay check. Am I also to assume that you won't be coming back to work your notice?"

"I would rather not if I'm honest Carol."

"Then I shall mark it as some of your holiday to avoid issues further up the chain and Anna. I know we haven't always seen eye to eye but I will miss you and I have always had a deep fondness for you, one so deep that I always deemed it inappropriate for work. Now that you're leaving maybe you would consider coming out for a drink with me?"

I silent choked on my end of the line, I didn't know whether to laugh or cry.

"Oh, Carol. That is very flattering but I am afraid that I could not possibly as my boyfriend gets very jealous," I lied and I hated lying but I didn't want to hurt her feelings.

"Well most men don't mind if it is another woman..."

On cue Xavier stormed into the room. "Who is that on the phone? I told you no phone calls without my permission. Are you cheating on me again, Anna, because I won't have it!"

I stifled a giggle as he winked at me and Carol coughed and spluttered down the phone. "Oh, er I see! Well best of luck in your new job or whoever you fancy doing. I mean find yourself doing. Goodbye, Anna."

"Bye, Carol, and thank you."

I hit the red phone and sat on the sofa with my mouth hanging open.

31

"So when's your date with Carol?" Xavier smirked before stepping back out of reach.

"Shut up, loser." I grumbled, pulling the blanket from under me wrapping my cold legs up.

"One down, one to go! You can do it Ace. Hopefully your landlady won't ask you on a date..." He darted back into the kitchen and closed the door.

My conversation with my landlady wasn't great. She had wanted me out from the beginning, claiming my ex-boyfriend Joseph had been staying over all the time and that a debt collector had turned up at the door. Apparently today she was going to ask me to leave anyway and that she had hated having me there. Well then, I had best go and collect my stuff. The only issue was that I didn't have any means of transport as my last beloved Audi A3 lost its clutch and I could not be bothered to fit a new one. I had cried when the scrap man took it but I only had myself to blame. I should have been bothered instead I used the money from the scrap yard for drugs. I wondered if I would be able to rent a van at this short notice and I wasn't even sure I could afford it.

"You need to move it all today?" Xavier waltzed back in.

"Yeah but I need to check what money I have and whether I can get a rental van or something."

"I will help you, I have a car. Let me just grab a shower and then we can go."

"Xavier?"

"Yeah?"

"Do you have a boyfriend? I know you said you prefer to be alone but I realised I had never asked you. If you do, won't they mind you having someone move into your house? Should I not meet him first so he knows that I'm not an axe wielding murderer?"

"He is in the army and he is on tour at the moment Anna so yes I will tell him but no he won't mind. He trusts my judgement and given that you are not another man, he will have even less reason to worry."

"Okay good." I felt stupid for even saying anything. I mean, I was very lucky to be given this opportunity but I had no idea that I was about to become homeless and that my boss had designs on me. My naivety was astounding sometimes. I needed to work on that, big time.

I found my leggings from the washing basket and sprayed them with his deodorant; they would do for the task at hand.

Xavier had a red Audi A3 similar to mine but it was a couple of years older. He charmed my landlady and packed the car himself. My stuff just fit and I was hidden under blankets with my feet in a washing basket as he drove away.

"Thank you."

"No dramas." He smiled and turned the radio up. Whitesnake's *Here I Go Again* was playing. How fitting. Xavier put his foot down as we reached the edge of town and more blankets fell over my head obscuring my view. I was completely blind going into a world with nothing but I had never felt more prepared or more ready. The fiend in my brain just wanted to get high all the time but my strength was growing and growing fast. I briefly wondered how people did it without support. How did they believe when no one believed in them?

My mind wanted the high of the first line and my heart loved to feel good. My inner battle must have been obvious to Xavier as he pulled the blanket back slightly so that he could see my face.

"You got this, Anna. You can do it."

Xavier helped to keep the door open and let some light in and I knew I would have to do it myself, that I should be doing it myself. Old memories tried to creep in and I pulled the blanket back over my head and sunk into the seat.

I didn't know what I wanted from my life. I had felt cursed with talents I didn't deserve to have. I never had to try at school, I was always just good at it. Anything that was put in front of me I could do well. How could anyone complain about being good at stuff? So many people just wanted to be good at even one thing. When you don't believe in yourself and when you don't truly believe that you are good at anything. Depression is one of the strangest emotions to understand. From an outsider's point of view you look selfish and no one can see why you keep making yourself worse. Your actions and words do not make sense to someone trying to help you and, for me, that black cloud seemed to be my only friend at times.

What I didn't realise is that it fed on my insecurities and lied to me about being my friend. It isolated me from my friends and from myself. I didn't know who I was. That black cloud tried to kill me three times. It lived in my head and twisted my thoughts and even controlled my limbs at points. Drugs numbed the black cloud and stopped it from thundering around in my head. Though the next day was hard I knew I read somewhere that coke made you skinny. I enjoyed depriving myself of nourishment and food. I enjoyed hurting my face and sinuses – damaging my body and chain smoking whilst high. Nothing felt as good as the first line, not the third gram or the room and music change. It wouldn't bring the first line high again. It was never the same and no matter how many times I blamed my tiredness or my environment or even the drugs themselves, it was just me. The cloud was strong and drugs made it stronger. This cycle needed something even stronger to break it. Whatever excuse I made or how I scoffed at other people in their normal lives, I was self-harming every which way I knew how to and it had to stop.

The car slowed to a stop and Xavier pulled the blanket back and looked into my eyes. "Don't spend too long in there without some back up." He tapped my forehead gently and unclipped my seatbelt. "Come on, the quicker we get this done the quicker you can be settled."

It was the last thing I wanted to do and the cloud was there watching my every move, dredging up past shit and blaming me for it. Yet I found that the physical exercise was good once I started moving and sorting. Cloud faded into the background once Xavier had shown me where I could put my things. One of the doors off the landing had a desk and a book shelf, he said this could be my office if I wanted it.

I had sold most of my belongings for drugs. All that we brought away was nothing important. I had a few things left like my guitars and saxophone and a couple of dog-eared poetry books. These I could not sell. I put Seamus Heaney and Ted Hughes up on the big shelf. They looked lost without the other books I had collected throughout my young years.

Chapter Five

I made three different piles out of my clothes: one for keeping, one for charity and one for the bin. I was disgusted at the amount of male clothing I had. I let myself go completely because I wanted to hide my body from the world. I could feel how men leered, even when I had just my arms out in a summer top. I felt it right to my core and I hated it. I wondered how long I would let other people's feelings and emotions take power over me. I carried my curse of empathy with my cloud and the three of us held hands and sat miserably on a roundabout in a kid's playground. There was no skipping here just put downs and scars on the forearm.

I looked at the clothes again. All the men's clothes went into charity and the boxer shorts into the bin. I had one black summer dress, a black halter neck bikini and my beloved black Superdry hoodie left. All my clothes were black.

"You need a hand with those?" Xavier called as I struggled down the stairs with bin bags.

"No, thanks. I've got this!"

"Alright. I'm just making some tuna sandwiches for

us."

"Thanks. I'll be done in five minutes or so." I set the bags for charity by the front door and took the other one out to the bin. Back upstairs I leant my guitars up against the wall and took my dress, bikini and hoodie through to Xavier's hanging rail. There were a couple of spare hangers and I slotted my clothes in amongst his. My bedding wasn't needed and it felt like old guilt and drug abuse so I wrapped it in a bin liner, keeping just one blanket. The blanket was from my gran but I felt nothing as I held it. No voice or memories came forward. It was as if I did not know her and, now she was gone, so were her memories. I put the other bag by the rest at the front door and took the blanket in to the washing machine.

"You hungry?"

"Yes."

"Wow! You actually want to eat? Good girl!"

"Yay." I scowled at Xavier as he rubbed my arm with encouragement. I had done enough churning over past and the cloud was struggling back in. I wanted to get high. I was hoping the tuna sandwich would suffice for now.

We ate in silence and I tried to look out the window to the mirror at the bottom of the garden but Xavier had other ideas about where my attention should be.

"So, now you've cleared through your stuff how do you feel?" Xavier pushed his plate away and set his strong forearms on the work surface.

"Better, but I want a line. Also it was a good idea at the time but now I only have one outfit."

"Well we best go to the shops this afternoon, then."

"I haven't any money and I also need to job hunt." I might be a druggie with nothing to give but I have some morals I can dust off.

"I can get you clothes."

"Nope. You could lend me your laptop for job hunting and printing off my CV though."

"Of course. I will get it for you." He dusted himself clean of crumbs and picked up our plates.

"Oh and, even though I've been kind enough to stay out of your head. I have told your mum that I will be bringing you home later on tonight."

"What? How did you get her number? Do you know how far it is?" I pulled a face. I was not what my mother wanted to see and even though she had no idea about my habits, I am pretty sure she had never been proud of me. I was a mess, fresh out of a failed relationship, with no aspirations.

Xavier returned with his silver MacBook in his hands. He passed it to me with a smirk and I knew I wasn't getting out of the road trip home.

A few hours later I had updated my CV and applied for what felt like fifty different jobs in town. I had twelve printed out CVs that ran two pages each. One of my female friends wanted to meet me in town for coffee so I agreed to meet her.

Chapter Six

"Hey, Anna! So good to see you!" Tash smiled and hugged me as I met her on the corner next to the library. I knew she had no one else to talk to about her mixed up life and she was going through a bad time. She needed to talk and I just listened to her while I handed out CVs in the local businesses that would accept them, data protection was a bitch these days.

The last place I went was a pub on the market square. Tash knew the guy who managed the place and she showed me the barrage of texts he sent her daily. He was excited to see her and eyed me carefully. We exchanged a bit of banter and Tash decided here would be where she wanted to have her coffee. I opted for water and we sat out the back of the pub by the bins. It was cobbled between the shops with no vehicle access but due to the pubs position, they were forced to have the bins next to the back seating area.

The hot autumn sun heated the big red container up and I was thankful that my sense of smell was slightly muted. The manager came out to chat Tash up and focussed on me a little, I needed a job so I switched my charm on. His name was Neil and he said he would be in touch.

I sat and helped Tash through her problems by giving her the advice and the belief she wanted from me. I gave her some of my light and she was happier. It was time for me to go back home, to my new home and then to my first home. Being out in town had drained me and Tash had drained me with her drama but at least for now she was happier. It wasn't her fault she couldn't see herself for what she really was but enough was enough and I needed Xavier. Another day I could help her to see how amazing she was inside of her insecurities.

"You called?" Xavier grinned at my shocked face. Where had he come from? He had got changed into fitted jeans, smart black shoes and a black shirt. My mouth went dry as I drank him in. His hair was tied back in its usual fashion and his sleeves were rolled up to reveal his tattoos on his forearms. Tash pushed me aside and introduced herself, whipping me with her hair as she flicked it seductively.

"He's gay, Tash," I muttered, stepping back as she continued to preen and bat her eyelashes at him.

He stepped away from her and grabbed my hand instead. "It was very nice to meet you but I need to get this lady home! We can meet properly another time. Take care!" Xavier pulled gently on my arm. I hugged Tash goodbye and walked off to the car.

Xavier had packed my few items of clothing and my blanket was on the front seat. I buried my face in the soft fabric and inhaled the delicious scent of summery fabric softener. He had washed and dried it for me, obviously knowing its sentiment or maybe he had been in my head and seen me as a child and my attachment to a white muslin cloth. I had taken it everywhere with me and it comforted me when I smelt it and now I was older and not able to take a cloth with me, I sought solace in my hood usually. When times were really bad I smelt its clean scent and it made everything go away. Xavier plugged his phone into the aux lead and sounds of Deaf Havana filled the car. I checked my phone and saw I had a message from Tash:

You should know, Anna, that he is definitely NOT gay.

I made a face and then snuck a look across at Xavier's profile. He was singing quietly to the music and concentrating on the road. He was hot, stupidly hot but she was just hoping he would be available. I knew what she was like with men and she would do anything to get her hands on him. I thought about it and I was okay with it. If she somehow managed to turn him not gay then she could have him.

I ignored the pit of green jealousy in my stomach as I knew, whatever happened, he would be gay as far as I was concerned.

Chapter Seven

My mum's house was a three hour drive away and it was
beginning to get dark. The clocks were due to go back in
a month's time and so the evenings still held a little light.
Summer wanted to stay and it was confusing going out in
a jumper but by mid-day feeling like you'd spent an hour
in the gym. The fields gave way to the motorway and I
saw the first star opposite the crescent moon. The hot
skyline and ink that fell upon it soothed my soul and I
could feel my light burn a bit brighter. There was so much
for me to learn but I wondered how much of it I already
knew, just like at school, maybe I could feel it in my
bones. Maybe my bones knew it all and I had to learn
how to listen. My phone buzzed again and it was Tash:

Neil wants to meet for an interview.

"Well done, sweetheart." Xavier murmured. By now
I was used to him being in my head. I knew he hadn't
taken his eyes off the road. I hoped he hadn't seen or felt
the other text from Tash.

I text her back to arrange a time for my interview and

I hoped that it would quell my aching sense of failure. We were taking the sea road. There was a quicker way along the country roads but the rawness from the nights spent with Joseph driving up and down that road would have been too much.

We would get high and then drive halfway up that route and sleep in a lay-by before continuing on to mum's for food. I believed we were in love and I adjusted to Joseph's lifestyle of the bare minimum. He wasn't qualified to drive but he would fight me for the driver's seat in my own car at every turn. I was exhausted and I couldn't battle him so I gave in and at each turn we lost. Every single thing that could go wrong went wrong.

He eventually robbed me and left me with nothing. Even after that I let him back in my life but he stole from me again and has now got another woman pregnant.

When I look back, I can't be sad and I can't try and rationalise it with black and white thinking. I knew deep down that people's behaviour was just an extension of themselves, as opposed to a reflection of his feelings towards me. Just as my feelings of inadequacy made me unable to accept love fully without wanting to pick holes after the day was done.

Joseph had supported me through one of the worst days I have ever experienced at my Gran's funeral and held my hand throughout. His heart was golden but he was too wrapped up in his childhood traumas and survival instincts to want a new way of life.

I remembered one night by the sea when I had new antidepressants and mixed them with alcohol. I wanted coke and I was chatting to people at the bar to get it. I had ignored Joseph for the last part of the evening and by rights he was angry. As soon as we stepped out the front door of the pub he started an argument.

I was distant and uncaring. The rain had started to fall in fat drops and lightening was crackling across the sea. I was not a fan of a storm but the way the lightening danced along the water and lit up the sky was something to behold. The thunder couldn't shake me into feeling and I walked ahead of him with my hood up, trying to call my friend. My flip flops slipped in the rain as my speed increased trying to get away from him. He kept shouting and I just wanted him to leave me alone. He managed to catch me and I pushed him away again.

He kept shouting that he loved me and I had to stop running away. I threw away the engagement ring that he made me after he slammed me in to the wet ground.

It bounced down a storm drain and I used the distraction to call my friend again. I wanted help; I was so afraid and he would not leave me alone. Joseph took my phone and snapped it in two. I pushed him away again but he wouldn't let me go. He wrapped a hand around my throat and drove me into the puddle on the floor.

In that moment I had wanted to die. I wanted him to leave me alone but he constantly trapped me. Later that night I tried to slit my throat but he found me and stopped me. I woke up with poppy dots up my neck and arms and deep purple bruises on my elbows and legs. I wore a scarf and trousers for the next four days in one of the hottest summers since records began.

It made me realise a lot. I blamed myself for it afterwards, which was one of my favourite pastimes. My head was so full of other people's feelings and versions of events that it was hard for me to string out who was wrong or right.

What I do believe is that Joseph loved me so much he couldn't stand to be away and when I wanted time alone he couldn't cope.

Life wasn't about pointing fingers; it was about understanding and I often got mad about being able to understand. It was tiring and it made me give a lot of people second, third and fourth chances when they did not deserve it.

Xavier's hand covered mine and he squeezed it reassuringly.

Would I be able to appreciate things to the level I did if I hadn't been through the things I had?

Something caught my eye out of the window. It was a light out to sea. I shook my head and looked again. I felt Xavier's attention shift in my direction and then back to the road. I could see a green orb hanging above the surface. It bathed the clouds above and the water below in a ghostly glow.

"What is that?"

"Probably just a trick of the light!"

"No, Xavier. I have twenty-twenty vision. What is that?"

"Honestly, Anna, it's just a smudge on the window. Just ignore it." He pulled his hair down and it fell softly on his shoulders. I couldn't be distracted by him. He knew what he was doing. I focussed again and it was still out there. It was big enough for me to still see it even though we had been driving at seventy-five miles per hour.

I could feel something in my hands, a buzzing of

energy as I kept my eyes fixed on it.

"Hey, lady, do you want to put some music on? I have Spotify Unlimited and you can put whatever you want on." Xavier handed me the phone from its cradle and I had to look at it. Once it was in my hands and I looked up for the orb again, it had gone.

I would have thought I had gone mad if I hadn't picked up on Xavier's hand raking through his hair. I moved so I could see his face and there was a small v between his eyebrows. He caught me looking and tried to flash me a dazzling smile but I knew something was up.

I looked down at his phone and scrolled aimlessly through the music. My mind usually went a mile a minute but what had I just seen… did I really see anything? For a small moment I wondered if I was going crazy and that maybe the drugs had taken their toll on my brain. I stuck some music on, some crap from the charts, and returned his phone to its holder.

The seascape had given way to dark trees splaying their long fingers across faded sky. I settled back in my seat and tried to switch off from it all.

"Are you hungry, Anna?"

"No."

"Don't go into your head and shut me out."

"I'm fine, just let me work it out. I'm coming from a very deep and dark hole and it will take time. Plus I seem to have done too many drugs and now I am crazy."

"You are not crazy, Anna. You just need time, like you said."

"I think I'll try and get some sleep if you don't mind."

"Of course." He turned the music off and I pulled the blanket around me.

Chapter Eight

I woke what felt like hours later and looked straight into Xavier's eyes. He unwrapped me from my blanket cocoon and unclipped my seatbelt.

"I'll get the bag. You go ahead, I'm right behind you."

"You know you can't be in my room with me if you're not my boyfriend, right?"

"I told your mum that I was so don't worry. It makes her feel safer for the time being as it gives her an understanding of what she thinks my intentions might be. We can clear it up in the future when you're better."

"But she doesn't know how sick I've been."

"I think parents always know more than they let on but I don't think she knows about your drug habit. Come on. Let's go in, Anna. It's cold out here." He gently pushed me forward towards the oak front door. It had been well-weathered and it squeaked in protest as I opened it.

"Darling! You're home!" Mum bustled into the hallway and gathered me up in a huge hug. I held back tears as I inhaled her lovely scent and wrapped my arms around her. I had missed her so much but I couldn't shake that feeling that I had let her down. I should have done more or been better for her. Especially as Granny was gone now. I drew back from Mum's embrace and glanced at Granny's old doorway in the corner of the room. The huge flag stones were warm under my feet with delicious under floor heating. Granny's little dog, Bluebell scurried in and jumped up at me with her tail wagging furiously. I bent down to fuss her and she licked my face, again I felt guilty for not being there for her and her little waggy tail. Bluebell had a shiny black coat with a little white patch on her chest and on one foot. She had been rescued from a place down in Cornwall and I think she was a Collie cross but no one was completely sure.

"Hello Hannah. I am Xavier. We spoke on the phone earlier." Xavier extended his hand to her but she bundled him into a hug. He towered over her petite frame but it was obvious who was in control.

"Come through and sit down. Are you hungry? Would you like a drink?"

"I'm fine, thank you, but a glass of water would be lovely." Xavier replied.

"Are you sure? I have just put the kettle on."

"Okay, tea would be great, thanks. White no sugar." Xavier took my hand and squeezed it. He was right to bring me home and even though my stomach was a swirling madness of guilt and fear of not being good enough, I loved my family and right now I needed them. I hadn't been home for almost half a year and I had only managed a few short phone conversations with Mum. I had briefly mentioned about Joseph leaving me and she had been angry on my behalf. I didn't want to bother her with my train wreck of problems and the pair of them had been more than accommodating for my failures.

"Dennis is in the sitting room. Go on through and say hi, sweetheart. I'll get you a tea with one sugar – you look like you need it." Mum filled the kettle up at the large butlers sink before putting it on the gas hob. The cooker always took a few clicks before it would light and even when you thought you had managed it, you had to hold the gas button in for a number of years to keep it going on its own.

Dennis was my stepfather and had been part of the family since I was four years old. I wasn't sure how he would behave towards me as I certainly hadn't matched up to my brother in success and I was coming home with nothing but debt. I held my breath as I walked into the sitting room and headed straight for the spare cream sofa that wasn't occupied by him or the cat.

"Hello, Anna. How are you? It's been a long time since we've seen you! You must be Xavier!" Dennis beamed and stood up to shake Xavier's hand. "This one looks better already." He winked at Xavier and my heart sank. I hated that I was lying to them about my relationship status and I knew they just wanted me to have someone kind to share my life with. That was all I really wanted. I did not want to let them down again with another failed relationship.

Xavier took a seat next to me and put his arm around my shoulders. Willow the cat jumped straight onto his lap and began purring contentedly. She was my little cat and she was beautiful with her long cream fur, grey diamond face and big blue eyes. She sniffed my hand and looked at me with contempt. I had been away too long, I didn't need her to tell me.

Xavier and Dennis got along well and they touched over a range of different subjects. I zoned in only to gratefully accept a steaming mug of tea from Mum. I could feel her eyeing me and trying to gauge where I was. I knew she possessed a deeper understanding than she let on, it must be where I got it from.

I wondered if I would be more forthcoming and feel part of the family if she showed a likeness to me. Maybe we just look for people to blame when we can't heal a part of ourselves that we don't understand.

"I know it is fairly early but it has been a long drive. Do you mind if we head off to bed?" Xavier asked my parents politely.

"Of course not! I left towels on your bed and Anna can show you where everything is!" Mum got up to hug us both and Dennis waved a friendly goodnight.

I headed to the upstairs bathroom and got ready for bed. I walked into my room and Xavier was sat on the bed gazing at a Nirvana poster on the wall. The rest of my room was cream; one of my best friends and I had got covered in paint in a redecorating fiasco. I put the Nirvana poster back up because the room felt wrong without it. My bedspread had been overhauled by Mum and her plain white spare sets. The carpet was new and also cream, it was safe to put a fresh one in now I was older and not living at home. I was very creative, even more so as a child. One time Mum had come down into the kitchen to find my brother, myself and the sitting room carpet covered in red paint.

I guess Mum had maybe gotten over it now and so I was allowed fresh, light colours in my room. Xavier smiled at me before sticking his foot out and pulling my hand so I tripped over and onto the bed as he got up.

"Get your head down. You'll sleep well at home."

He wandered off to the bathroom and I quickly got into some old pyjama shorts and a t-shirt that I found stuffed in a drawer. They smelt a little musty but they would have to do.

I laid down facing the wall in my favourite spot. There was a slight dent in the mattress from all my years sleeping here. I heard the door latch click shut and the bed dip slightly as Xavier climbed in beside me. He turned the bedside light off and wrapped a strong arm around my waist. I quietly wondered how fat I seemed at this angle and started to worry.

"Go to sleep, Anna. You have nothing to worry about," he mumbled into my hair. It didn't take me long to fall into a deep sleep with his warmth around me.

I dreamt of our farm just down the road, Granny and I were digging a hole in the top field. She wanted to plant a red oak for Granddad, who had died when he was young. I had never met him but I knew him. He was the voice of reason as I grew up. He looked after me and sat with me in my head when I was alone. He was my guide and you could see he was still here on the farm, the rustle of wind through the trees and the tiny orbs in every picture I took here. Granny leant on her spade and she was telling me how she was still here and she loved me very much. We kept digging in companionable silence under the warm sun.

I woke up smiling as it felt like she was really still here but as the morning fog lifted from my hazy brain, the cold hands of grief wrapped around my heart again.

I had spent most of my childhood with Granny. I never felt like I belonged to this family but I belonged to her. We would go for long walks in the summer heat and work on the farm together. She was my person. She was my only person and sometimes I had been too blind to see it. After she died I had wasted time thinking she didn't love me and, when I walked into her home, I saw that I was everywhere. It was covered with notes and letters from me. My self-doubt wouldn't allow me to see that I was her person too. Silent tears slid down my face as I looked over at the little teddy bear she had bought me. When you pressed its belly it played *You Are My Sunshine*. I leaned over to grab it and hold it close to my face and I pressed its belly, hoping that it might make her come back to me.

Xavier stirred and light blue eyes looked sleepily up at me. He pulled me back to him and held me whilst I let my grief out. I know they say that time is a healer but I seemed to go from numb to devastated and each time that sadness came it was just as powerful. The periods of numbness lasted longer and longer and as I tried to make the right choices to improve my life it got a little easier. I wanted nothing more than for Granny to be proud of me. I never had the chance to show her marriage or children or even buying a house. She only saw my spiral of depression and moodiness towards the end. I hoped she could see me trying and I hoped that, wherever she was, she and Granddad were together and most of all, that she was happy.

Chapter Nine

I could hear Mum buggering around outside on the landing. I knew she wanted me to get up and see her. When I opened my door she feigned innocence and pretended she hadn't been trying to wake me up with her noise making.

"Hello, darling. Lovely day isn't it?"

"No questions in the morning, Mum, you know that!"

"Well, it is late."

"What time is it?"

"... eight"

"That's very late isn't it?" I gave her a playful push and walked towards the bathroom but she ran in there first. "Come on Mum, I need a wee."

"Well that's awkward. It would appear that I was here first." She pulled her pants down and sat on the toilet.

"I bet you don't even need a wee!" I grumbled and waited on the landing.

"I might read my new book whilst I'm in here..."

"Stupid."

"You're stupid." She giggled. It had become a thing to elongate the word stupid when someone did something particularly stupid. This came from a time when she had shut Dennis' hand in the car window and he had shouted stupid in a very stupid way.

Xavier peeped out of my doorway to see what was going on and laughed at me stood there with my hair in a mess and a scowl on my face.

"Cross your legs, Anna. It helps when you need a wee."

"You can shut up as well." I mumbled and I heard more giggling from the toilet. "Can we make sure the door is shut when we have outside guests here Mum? I am sure Xavier does not want to walk in on you in there."

"Well, he might like it."

"Stupid." I shook my head in embarrassment and Xavier winked at me.

"Anyway what is an 'outside guest'?" Mum asked.

"I don't know. Someone that has come from outside and isn't used to your behaviour?"

"But surely that is just a normal guest?" I could hear her flushing the toilet and washing her hands.

"No, because I am a guest but not an outside guest. Look, just leave it. Can I wee now?"

Mum was right beside me. "The toilet is only for outside guests." She stuck her tongue out at me before doing a silly walk down the stairs.

"I think she might have missed you, Anna." Xavier smiled before pushing past me and into the bathroom.

"What the hell? I was queuing!" My indignant remark was met by laughing from both Xavier and Mum. They were having far too much fun for this time of the morning. There was a toilet downstairs but I preferred the upstairs bathroom and its giant velux window. If you weren't careful, you banged your head on the eave space that hung over the bath but it was so lovely and light in there. You could see way across the other farm fields and, at night, the sky that twinkled with stars. For the first time I felt that it was good to be back.

Chapter Ten

Xavier walked out into the first field ahead of me. The autumn sun shone through his blond hair as he took another step forward into the crunchy white frost. The hawthorn was laden with red fruit amongst its wicked thorns. Its ripe berries stood proudly next to the jealous sloe bush. I should really make some more sloe gin but I didn't have the taste for picking the sour blue berries. Granny and I would pick them every year and the old bread bags bulged with our harvest. I remember one particular year; we picked through the back of the orchard and I pulled a stem of giant hogweed out of our way before I realised what I had put my hand on. Luckily it was dead but it didn't stop the phantom itch burning across my palm every so often as we sat down for earl grey tea.

"She's here," Xavier murmured as the wind moved gently across the long grass. It looked like it was breathing and alive as it danced this way and that across the long meadow. I could feel her too along with unbridled joy and a happiness I hadn't felt before so I knew it couldn't be mine. Without thinking, I put my hands out in front of me and the energy flowed to my palms and the wind whipped around my ears.

"Hello, dear." Granny's voice sounded in my head and a tear slid down my face.

Xavier smiled at me encouragingly. "You made this happen, Anna. She is here for you."

A sad smile lifted to mirror his but it didn't quite make it. I wished she was here to hug me and so I could see her face again. I wished she would hold my arm as we ambled across the fields together and I wished that she would rest her arm through mine and stroke my wrist and absentmindedly play with whatever bracelet I had chosen to wear. The wind whistled around me and enveloped me in a hug. It was bizarre how such a naturally cold element felt so warm.

"Anna, I don't think you understand what you are capable of." Xavier's eyes were loud and wide. The wind grew stronger before suddenly stopping. I hadn't realised my eyes had been shut until he had spoken. "Your love for her is so strong, she can still feel it where ever she is."

"But that's the same as anyone who has lost a loved one. You hear countless stories of them coming through and contacting them in some form or another."

"You have no idea, sweetheart. You really don't."

"So tell me what is down the bottom of your garden then."

"It's just a mirror," he said flatly.

"And what of the green ball of light over the sea last night?"

"When you give up strong drugs it makes you see funny things and some people can hallucinate really badly." His chin was jutted upwards and his eyes stern. I clearly would not be getting anywhere with questions. I would have to figure it out for myself. I didn't need his help anyway.

"Don't do that. Don't make that face."

"What? I haven't done anything!"

"That shutting down face. You usually have the open, chance giving face and now you have your walls up and shut down face on. Don't shut me out."

"I'll do what I want actually, I have done all my life and will continue to do so as and when it suits me."

"Do not be stubborn."

"Try me." I flashed my eyes at him and the wind took off again, this time right in his face and blasted his perfect hair back. I smirked and showed him another one of my favourite faces, the 'try me' face.

"You are so much like her, you don't even know." Xavier smiled and I wondered how the hell he knew that and how the hell did he know her. He could only be two years older than me at maximum.

"How old are you?" I demanded, stepping closer to him and studying his attractive face. His smile grew broader and shiny white teeth bared themselves to me.

"Does it matter? I think you might have seen enough of the world to know we can have friends of all ages and walks of life."

"Must be an old man then." I stepped back and giggled. He took a step forward to swipe playfully at me but I was too fast.

The wind played with me and ran alongside me as I pounded one foot in front of the other through the damp grass. The heavy sun had thawed odd patches through the middle of the field but the edge stayed crisp and white. My breath fell into an easy rhythm as I settled into a good running pace. I had missed this. I had missed the power of my limbs working and pumping as my breath clouded in condensation behind me. I was like lightning, like a tiger that couldn't be tamed.

Xavier pounced on me from behind and tackled me to the floor, tickling me mercilessly. I couldn't help the laughter but I loathed being tickled. It was torture to me and he had me on my back, his laughter joining mine across the quiet meadow. His eyes were beautiful, especially in this long sun with nature humming with energy all around us. If his eyes were beautiful then that must mean mine were too.

We locked eyes for a little too long and what? What was that? Was it a moment? No surely not. He was gay and well I... I was stupid as we had discovered this morning. He coughed and stood up briskly. Was he? No he couldn't be. Oh but he was, he was flustered! Oh what a sight to behold; the unruffled man was now ruffled. I laughed out loud, the loudest laugh I had in a long time. I was treated to a big scowl as he dusted imaginary dirt from his jeans.

Chapter Eleven

The walk round the rest of the farm did me a lot of good. They say laughter is the best medicine and I would not hesitate to agree but if everyone felt the way I did when I was in nature then they would know that was the best medicine. I am sure if you wanted to sit there and work out the scientific explanation for my happy emotions and look at the exercise and fresh air releasing my endorphins then you would find it.

This was more than just that, I felt like the old crap was releasing slowly, seeping out of every pore and I knew that I was finally safe to be me. It wasn't just going to happen overnight but it definitely did help to know that I had someone; even if it was one person I had only known a short while. Someone who understood me and accepted me for what I was, even under this broken facade. I had always asked the universe for someone like me to come along but I had usually visualised him being a romantic part of my life.

This was better. This was a million times better. I had enough men in my life just wanting to sleep with me but to have someone on this level who saw me for who I really was and didn't run away screaming... Well maybe I should treat myself better. How could I get annoyed at all the people that wanted to be with me or be my friend? All those people that relied on me or came to me for advice, surely that was a compliment but it made me angry and stupid. I couldn't cope with it and it took up too much of my time. Maybe it was just me who took up my time with thoughts that ran round and idiocy.

"You're getting lost in there again, aren't you?" Xavier stopped to observe the stunning view. A few fluffy white clouds had appeared in the blue azure sky and it seemed to go on forever and ever as if there was no space beyond it and the stars were just another slide that clicked over as the sun got tired. My cloud was nowhere to be seen. Xavier rubbed his forehead in understanding and smoothed his thick hair back into a pony tail.

"This amount of intelligence cannot be shared with everyone, Xavier. It isn't good to make people realise their stupidity." I smirked and he looked at me aghast.

"Anna! You bitch!"

"Why thank you, it's been a while since someone called me that and do you know what? It feels good!" I laughed as he punched me lightly on the arm.

"Seems like you're getting the hang of it now. Come on, let's get back, I am starving!"

"Oh shit yeah! I forgot Mum was doing roast beef!" We raced each other down the hill and through the valley along the side of the busy stream. A few deer bolted from the woods as we splashed through the water and up the boggy bank.

Granny and I had once sat for hours waiting for the

kingfisher that had been sighted once before. A good few 'squashed fly' biscuits and a flask of tea later we had decided to give up and come back another day. I think a little mouse had accidentally burrowed his way to the bank of the stream and foxed us into thinking it was a kingfisher's nest.

Xavier made it to the top of the steep hill before me. Even though the earlier run was great, I was still shaking off years of smoking and drug abuse and my lungs were desperately trying to recover.

After the amazing roast dinner of beef cooked in a mustard crust and goose fat roast potatoes with vegetables grown in the garden, we sat and watched a bit of Countryfile, I was almost asleep on the sofa when Xavier shoved me.

"I think it's time you went to bed."

I said my goodnights to Mum and Dennis and thanked them again for dinner. Xavier told me to go on up and he would be there soon.

It wasn't long after I had got into bed that he joined me and we settled into our new but normal sleeping positions. I hadn't once questioned it and, to be honest, maybe I was a body of safe comfort to him whilst his partner was away in the army. Was that so wrong to seek comfort in the arms of someone else where there was no sexual attraction? The fact that I was questioning it answered loud and clear. I lay under the small section of neon stars stuck to the ceiling, I couldn't get them off and had just painted around them when redecorating. Xavier tightened his arm around my waist and snuggled his head into my shoulder. His warmth was mollifying and I snuck a look at his face as he slept soundly. I wasn't ready for loving anyone. I had too much to do and too much to heal. Joseph had knocked the wind out of me and I needed to get back up again and do all those things I wish I had started a long time ago.

It was easy to blame Joseph for my lack of inspiration and drive but no one forced me to do anything. It was all down to me and I wanted to give Xavier all the credit for pushing me onto the right path. Maybe I shouldn't take it all on my shoulders. That was definitely one of my downfalls. I couldn't take help from anyone and set far too high standards for myself. I would then trip over these standards and end up self sabotaging because I couldn't achieve. I wanted to do everything at once and have it all now. Patience and delayed gratification were things I needed to learn. I was learning slowly and having stripped back all of my life now, I was able to see what I wanted. I might never fully know what I truly want but I needed to start somewhere instead of making excuses.

I decided to make a list of goals and my brain started firing off with different ideas and organisation. I glanced at Xavier's pretty face again and he was out for the count. I slid his arm off my tummy and scooted down to the end of the bed and over to my desk. I clicked the dusty lamp on and moved my memories box onto the floor. I had left some old drawings in the top drawer of the desk and they would suffice for making lists. I loved a list. I felt some of my old synapses firing up in my brain.

I knew it was up to me if I wanted to get good at life again. Being an adult was harder than I think any of us anticipated. Things in life came and went and if you didn't remain chilled out and open to these variations then you got stuck and sick.

I needed to embrace myself and my quirks. The page didn't take long to print as I wrote down my goals. These goals had been stuck inside for fear of rejection and failure. I felt hope and light shining through my darkness. The cloud was fading fast but he still loomed overhead, waiting for my self-doubt to rear its ugly head. I had forgotten that my inspiration usually struck around midnight and suddenly I wanted to start my goals. Mum's old laptop was sat under some of her old magazines in the corner. She had moved onto a tablet and her laptop had been sat in the dark in my room. It whirred noisily as I fired it up and I shot a worried look over to the softly snoring lump in my bed. There was no movement and I waited silently for another snore. When it came I breathed out and typed in the password. The laptop took a while to fully load and I couldn't blame it for sulking after being neglected for all this time. It still had Word on it from many moons ago when it was mine at university.

Once it had finally loaded my fingers hesitated over the keys and I bit my lip in uncertainty. What would I write about? What could possibly be so interesting in my life?

That self-doubt crept in again as I mulled over my lack of options on what to write and then I remembered my university lecturer's golden rule for writing. Always write about what you know because that will make the best writing. Maybe if I wrote down the past year of my life it could help me. I started tapping away at the keys gingerly. Suddenly it was like unravelling a ball of yarn and each hit on the black and white letters pulled more of the tight knot loose from inside of me. My shoulders sagged slightly lower as I let out my inner turmoil onto the blank page. My fingers beat out a steady rhythm that soothed my soul. I was in my bubble and I didn't need anyone else in it. I could create and manipulate my past, present and future. I had all the power in my hands and mind and, once I got started, I couldn't stop.

Chapter Twelve

It must have been around three a.m. when I felt warm hands on my shoulders. "Hey, Anna, have you slept yet?" Xavier murmured sleepily.

"Not yet, man. I just started writing and I haven't stopped."

"I'm pleased, sweetheart. I really am."

"I have written so much and I didn't even realise the time!"

"I'm just headed for the bathroom but when I get back you best have saved that work and be in bed. You need some sleep as well as success, Anna!"

"Alright. You know best," I grumbled, saving my work. I couldn't resist a read through it and I heard the door close gently behind Xavier as he re-entered the room. He wrapped his strong arms around my waist and threw me onto the bed. He made sure my work was saved and closed the lid of the laptop before tucking me in and sneaking his arms around me. I hadn't realised how jaded I was and soon I was drowsy with tiredness. As I drifted off I noticed the winking blue light flashing at me from the desk. It was my laptop reminding me there was still work to be done but we could both be on sleep mode for now.

I was awake before Xavier and I let the memories of the previous day drift deliciously in. The cold air drifted in through cracked open window. I always had a window open as I loved a cold room with a warm bed. The air at home felt much thicker than where I lived. The thickness was lung filling oxygen created by the wealth of nature around. A slight pain was forming around my eyes and in my nose. I guessed the colder bite that accompanied the morning frost was responsible for my pains but I knew it was related to my bad habits. I would be foolish to think I would get out of a heavy cocaine habit without some fallout. The cravings wouldn't be the only issue I had to face. For one thing, I would have a bigger appetite and my curves did not need any more nourishment. The thought started to trigger salivation over the white powder and the incessant need to feed my coke hunger. The cloud zoomed in gleefully as my tired mind tried to scheme how I could satisfy my need. The laptop blinked at me through the gloom and I climbed over a sleeping Xavier and towards the encouraging beacon on my desk. I pulled Xavier's hoodie off the floor and over my head. It was a lot colder closer to the open window and without my human hot water bottle.

Later that day we said our goodbyes to Mum and Dennis. I was always sad to leave them but I knew this time I would come back again with achievement and happiness. Mum's old laptop was tucked safely on the back seat with

Xavier's bag. I had also managed to find a couple of dresses at home and Mum had given me her grey cashmere sweater and £20 to get some tights and ladies underwear.

As Xavier pulled off the drive I saw a collection of small silver orbs in the side mirror. I shook my head and looked again, they were still there and glittered in the sun. The longer I looked the more connected I felt to them. This time I didn't mention anything to Xavier and he appeared not to have noticed. A knot formed in my stomach as I wondered how I had let Xavier get so close to me when I didn't know him at all. It was obvious that he was keeping something from me and something pretty big by the looks of it. I decided to keep the silver orbs a secret.

I kept checking the side mirror on the journey home but I never saw them again. Part of me didn't want to see them whilst I was sat next to Xavier. I revelled in having something of my own that no one could take away. I usually wore my heart and mind on my sleeve and felt it was just part of my makeup but now I realised I did it for some form of self validation.

The house was dark as Xavier manoeuvred the car with ease onto the gravel. Tomorrow I had my meeting at the pub and after the long drive I just wanted to climb in to bed. Xavier carried the bag in behind me and we headed straight up the stairs. I climbed into bed after brushing my teeth and pulling one of his oversized t-shirts on. He looked at me sideways as I puffed up my pillow and settled down beside him. "Anna. I need to confess something to you."

"Go on..."

"I have strong feelings for you and I've been trying so hard to keep it to myself but I just can't anymore."

"What? I thought you had a boyfriend?"

"Nope. I knew you didn't need any pressure or another man just trying to get with you and I assure you that I am not that guy."

"But you're gay."

"No Anna I'm not and I am so sorry for lying to you."

"Okay." My mind was whirring with so many questions but my instinct was laughing at me. My instinct knew all along but my self-doubt stopped me from accepting it. Xavier was looking at me reproachfully and I looked right back at him. All I could manage was a slightly raised eyebrow. A slow smirk turned his mouth. He pulled me closer to him and wound his hand into my hair. His lips were inches from mine and I could feel his smile.

"Anna, you don't know how badly I have wanted this. Laying next to you every night and holding your beautiful body and smelling your hair. I can't wait to taste you and feel you." His lips found mine and I was lost in him. His hands roamed over my bare thighs and my brain started to go into overdrive. How come I had managed to get into bed with this hot man? I was at my most vulnerable and also had a couple of spots on my bum. Shit his hand was there. Shit.

"Anna, stop. I think you're so hot. Stop over thinking and just enjoy the moment," he murmured into my mouth. His other hand found the hem of my t-shirt and he eased it slowly up my body and over my head. His mouth paved a trail down my neck and to my breasts. My back arched as he found what he wanted and he growled gently as he pulled my underwear off. He slowly moved in between my legs and slid inside me. God he felt good. I climbed higher and higher as he upped his pace and he called my name out as we came together.

Then he was gone, literally vanished into thin air. I sat up and looked around the room from my post orgasm haze. There was no sign of him at all. One minute he was there between my legs, coming with me, and then suddenly he was gone. What the fuck?

I laid down, hoping it was a dream and that I would wake up next to him. It took all my power to not search for my phone and call my dealer. Something of this magnitude had my skin crawling with need. I knew in my heart that it was wrong and after a long night of tossing and turning, I finally managed to fall into a long and dreamless sleep.

Chapter Thirteen

When I woke up the bed was big, too big. The events from the night before came flooding in and first one, then the other, my sleep sticky eyes opened wider and wider.

I searched the house for Xavier but I knew he wasn't here. One of the silvery orbs had managed to get into the house and it helped me search. At this point I would take all the help I could get and not question where it came from. Wild thoughts ran through my mind and I just couldn't make sense of it. Over breakfast I mused and I wanted to succumb to cloud and his evil grin. The orb sparked at cloud and whizzed around my head. I had my interview today and I needed to pull myself together. I couldn't explain where Xavier had gone and maybe I was missing something.

Maybe he had been a figment of my imagination I had created to save myself. Maybe I had to do it that way so I would get out of the self-destructive patterns I locked myself in. Maybe I had somehow managed to get this house, car and ever growing self-respect from somewhere by myself. If that was the case then I needed to be proud of myself, really proud of myself. Yes, Xavier might have seemed real, so real and I knew it was a very odd way of getting out of drugs and bad decisions but it seemed to work well. Already I missed him but I had to get on with my life and make sure I learnt from this. My sinuses were killing me today and one of my ears was tweaking with pain, just like the kind you get before an ear infection.

I breathed the steam in from the shower, hoping it would soothe the fire in my face. I threw on my black dress and one of the black shirts on the hanger. They must have been mine from my bloke phase along with my long board and two wetsuits on the rail. For the first time I wished I had some makeup to enhance my features. I opted for plucking my eyebrows and dark hairs on my upper lip. I tamed my thick curls with a hair brush and surveyed myself in the mirror. I would do for now but I needed to make the most of the £20 Mum gave me and get some new underwear and tights.

It was very brisk out in the open without any leg coverage but I needed to start being who I wanted to be. I wanted to wear dresses all the time and be a proper girl. I walked past Xavier's car and felt a pang of sorrow. I might have made him up in my head but I missed him, especially as we had taken it to the next level. I realised how crazy that sounded but my sexual beast had awoken inside and it was ready for more.

I shook my head and hurried down the street. It was another beautiful autumn day and the sun was warming me up as I walked into my new life. I was completely alone and for the first time I wasn't afraid anymore.

A blonde girl wearing all black saw me to a seat

downstairs in the pub. I had got a little sweat on during my fast walk and my thighs stuck to the leather. I shifted uncomfortably as she headed back over with some sparkling water. I nodded politely and thanked her.

Half an hour later and Neil finally came down the stairs. He pumped my hand briefly before eyeing my legs and asking me to go with him upstairs. It was even hotter up here and I sat on the edge of the seat to let whatever breeze might exist, blow up my skirt. I was trying not to focus on the sweat on my upper lip as he asked me questions and flirted. I needed this job and so I switched my charm on. I knew I could get a job based on my skills alone, I was a hard worker and I had climbed many steps on the career ladder. This job wasn't my be all and end all but it would suffice and I enjoyed charming people. He was such a scuzz ball, with his drooling over anything with a pulse, and for the first time was glad I had a dress on. I stealthily wiped my upper lip from sweat and leant forward, being extra careful to rest my boobs on my arm at the table. His eyes swelled at my swells protruding out the top of my dress.

"So, Anna, just to let you know that you won't be working with me. I have been asked go to another pub. You will have a new manager and I cannot guarantee that he will want to take you on but I will employ you and your first shift will be with him."

"Okay. No dramas. What do you need of mine? Bank details?"

"Yeah if you've got a bank card and some ID on you I can scan it in now."

"Okay, thank you." I handed over my cards and

waited for him to come back with the paperwork. I signed up for an eight hour contract but was assured that I would be given a lot more hours than that.

I smiled at the blonde girl as I walked down the stairs and out onto the square. The cold air was a relief from the sweatbox pub and I wondered what the hell I was going to wear to work. I think you would still be too hot in a bikini and I definitely was not going to be wearing one of those unless it was under my dress.

I wandered across the square, not in a massive hurry to get home. I knew I could be good at this successful thing but it was hard to keep it up all the time. Now I had a job and there would be new people in my life. Whatever reason Xavier had manifested meant something and even though I wanted to turn back and celebrate with drugs, what I wanted most of all was to tell him and see his handsome face light up and feel his arms around me.

"It's okay, Anna, I am always with you. Well done, baby." I turned around expecting to see his tall frame and long blond hair but he wasn't there. I had to remind myself he was just in my head. He was just an imaginary friend.

I decided to wander to TK Maxx before heading home but the crowds of people made me freeze at the doorway. Large crowds of people drained me as I felt all of their mixed energies. I knew I needed to do a food shop and get those pants and tights I promised myself but I was now not in the mood. Plus how far could I really stretch that twenty quid.

The house seemed very large when I shut the front door behind me. I put on another record of Xavier's, no,

I forgot, I meant mine. It might have explained why he had exactly the same eye colour as me. I loved eyes but I loved the colour of mine the best if I am truly honest. Maybe when my mind manifested him it made his eyes the colour of mine so I would trust him quickly.

AC/DC rocked through the sound system and it was literal music to my ears how good the quality was. I jigged into the kitchen, slightly tripping on the edge of the door frame as I travelled through. I checked through the cupboards, for some reason not knowing what I had in them. I came across the pasta that was had the other night for dinner. It was in a Tupperware and labelled with my name on it. The writing wasn't in my usual cursive but I guess if my brain was clever enough to work out a whole other person then it would be clever enough to make their writing different. I heated the food up in the microwave and retired to the kitchen island to eat. It was twilight outside and the dark night shadows had started to move and dance, a lot better than I could. I wondered how many shadows I had. Previously when walking I had only noticed one but the bushes and plants in the garden seemed to have two or more. Was I just a one hit wonder with one shadowy follower?

I was pushing the last bit of pasta around my blue Tupperware when a glint from outside flashed into the house. I looked up and saw the mirror twinkling at the end of the garden. The overhead kitchen light was reflecting in it and offered explanation but it still had me at the back door with breath fogging up the glass. I wanted to go to the mirror and see what it had hidden inside it but I remembered Xavier's warning to stay away.

The silver orb from this morning zoomed in from the sitting room and hovered by my side. We both decided to leave it for tonight. It was dark and, as hard as I tried not to be, I would always be scared of the dark.

I dumped my Tupperware into the sink and padded upstairs. The record player had played its last song and it reminded me why I loved vinyl so much. I could sit for hours and list reasons to love it but I loved how it knew when to stop playing, when enough was enough and it left you with the right amount of wanting.

I had placed Mum's laptop in the office and after a relaxing bath I sat in front of it and bought it to life. I got lost in my writing and I could think of no better way to get my mind off the day's events. I never told anyone what I wrote about, it was mine and mine alone. I think we all need that alone time switch off that no one else should know about. I had forgotten how I settled as I wrote and a small budding sense of satisfaction built slowly. At this moment I did not want anyone else to be around me. I didn't need anyone. It was nice to share but I think I needed some alone time and that was great because that was all I had now Xavier was gone.

If he was ever here

I fired off a text to Mum to let her know that I got the job and got ready for bed. I noticed a slip of paper on the bedside table that had not been there this morning. It was in the same cursive as the label on my pasta and it said:

Anna, I am still here. Find me.

Wow, maybe I was really sick. I made a mental note to call the doctors in the morning. I thought there might be a fall out from the cocaine withdrawal but I didn't think hallucinations were part of it. At least it had been a pleasant distraction.

I snuggled into bed and buried my face in the pillow he slept on. It smelt of Xavier.

How could that be?

I hadn't even questioned the orbs, especially not the one that was hanging around me. Was I just going insane or was there something bigger happening?

Maybe it wasn't the doctors I needed to call but rather the spiritual church up on Red Brick Lane.

Chapter Fourteen

The next morning I made a request for a call back from the doctors as, surprise, surprise, they did not have any appointments. My research also showed that the spiritualist church was open this evening for a healing circle. I didn't start work until midday and so I had a whole morning to do some investigating. The note had completely disappeared from the side where I left it. I looked under the bed and behind the bedside table. It was nowhere to be seen.

Downstairs in the kitchen I made toast and slathered some Marmite on it, all the time eyeing the shiny mirror at the bottom of the garden. Xavier told me not to go down there. He told me I wasn't ready. I shouldn't go down there. I should just stay up here eating my toast and get on with my life. Yeah, Xavier was right, I thought as I put on my shoes and unlocked the door. I really should stay in the house. I was already past the dahlias and half way to the mirror. Orb was whizzing with excitement and it must be time that he had a name. Toad, I would call him Toad. Toad buzzed around my ear and this time I listened.

The grass was wet and it darkened my already black

shoes. A shot of adrenaline surged through me as I finally got to the mirror. I could hear faint whispering and there was twitching in the grass in front of it. Toad flew up higher as if he didn't want to face the mirror. I stepped right up to it and swore out loud. I could see myself floating with white light around me. My hair was long, just how I had always wanted it before I kept dying it and cutting it. I was wearing white leggings bare feet and a white vest top (I never wore white. I just had to look at it and it was dirty.) A long silver necklace hung around my neck and down between my boobs. It was circular, with markings on it like craters on the moon. I pawed at my chest but the chain wasn't really there and I wasn't the same version of me in the mirror. I couldn't stop looking and suddenly I felt a hand on my shoulder and Xavier appeared in the reflection behind me.

"Anna, I need you."

"How are you here again?"

"I am real and you know it, you just have to accept that someone could exist that is right for you."

"I'm going to the doctors later. I need to..."

"Just be careful, Anna. What you tell them can frighten them. People that do not understand something can have nasty reactions to it. Do not let anyone dumb you down because they cannot understand your power or that they feel threatened by you. I've told you before, Anna. You are special and not just to me."

"What if I am going mad though, Xavier? You just disappeared after we had sex. I know some men do that but to literally vanish into thin air? How do you even do that?"

"I don't know but you have to keep believing in yourself and come and find me."

"How the hell do I find you?"

"I don't know that either but the more you believe, the closer you will get. I told you not to come down here but you never listen. This time I am grateful, very grateful, that you believed in yourself enough to come down here and trust your instinct."

"If you're not really here right now then how come I can feel your hand?"

"It's something that the mirror does. I don't understand the mirror either but its showing you how. It showed me you and helped me to figure out how to find you." His hand moved across to my heart and it quickened under his touch. "Just trust your instinct and follow the signs. Go to the church tonight and if you ask for help then it will come."

"Why would they make me responsible for a task like this?"

"Who are they? Anna, you're different from others but there isn't some council for different people that sets you up with tasks. If you want to find out your purpose then you go looking but if you don't then you stay where you are."

"Okay. All right. I will go later to the church."

"Anna, one last thing..."

"What?"

"I miss you and your sexy ass." He grabbed a fistful of my hair and kissed my neck. I leant back into him and he was gone again. The mirror's image faded but the necklace hung heavy down my chest. I had two choices now and if I thought too much then I would take the wrong path. Don't think just feel.

I closed the back door behind me and the necklace felt heavier the further away I walked from the mirror. My brain started to whir with over thinking and indecision but I silenced it. I could not go on this way. I had the chance to get the best thing I had ever had back and was I going to let my doubts hold me back anymore? Not a chance. If he wasn't real and this was all in my head then it should be entertaining at the least. Having lost everything, I didn't have any excuses to not pursue this quest. I must admit I was disappointed that my quest didn't ride in on the back of a unicorn but I wasn't complaining at feeling Xavier's touch again. I settled down on the sofa and put Ben Howard on the record player. It wasn't long before my eyelids grew heavy. I hadn't been up long but I suspected the lack of drugs was fuelling my fatigue.

My sleep was full of vivid images of another world, it looked just like this one but I knew it wasn't here. When I awoke I felt unsettled and I had savage heartburn. I raided the cupboard in the bathroom and found some indigestion tablets. They were the little flavoured ones I had when I was a child. Ever since I could remember I had problems with my stomach, finally I managed to get an appointment for an endoscopy and they found a hiatus hernia. My illness explained my stomach issues and there was no quick fix. The operation only lasted for a few years and I believed that I could fix it on my own if I tried hard enough. The stomach was positioned right where you received energy from other people, aka, the solar plexus. It was no wonder I suffered with health issues as I could not protect myself from taking on everyone's energy and I couldn't work out how to deal with it.

I looked at my phone and I had a missed call and a voicemail from the doctors. I decided to long it off and see what happened at the church instead. Xavier had been right about most things so far and I knew they would foist some form of medication on me. That was something I really did not need.

Chapter Fifteen

I walked to work with a pair of black headphones. I had found them in one of the beside drawers. There was something to be said for headphones as opposed to earbuds. All the noise was blocked out and I could fully focus on the music. I had stuck on one of my old playlists as I was walking out the door without thinking and Kaleo filtered through with Danny's favourite song *All The Pretty Girls*.

Oh Danny. I had known him for just over three years now and what a rollercoaster it had been. He had been the false 'one' the guy who keeps coming back after each failed relationship and the one you can never say no to. He had broken my heart time and time again but I just couldn't stay away.

I had met him when I was working in a pub in a town twenty miles from here. He still lived in the pretty medieval town. I didn't know where he was though. He would never tell me where he lived and his excuse to that was that I had never asked him. I knew a little more about his whereabouts towards the end, before I had enough. In the third and final year he came with me when I had to collect a PA system from Wales. I was sure he only came with me as it was his home country but he made the day special, or what I thought was special. He said he was sorry for everything he had done in the past but that he was here for me now. He put his arm around my shoulders and I didn't know what to do with myself.

Danny had bought chocolate and some drinks for the road trip. I didn't think that much of it. Each song I put on he knew and sang along to. He had a good voice and it was so refreshing to be able to sing with someone. When we were together it felt like I had my person, my person on my level. He held my hand for a little when we were sat in the van and I couldn't get enough of his touch. It took me back to the first time he stayed over three years ago…

We had been out drinking and dancing all night and he had danced me in to a stupor. A Queen song had come on in the bar and he had dragged me on to the dance floor. He would pull me in close and twirl me away again before dropping to the floor and running his hands up my legs and grabbing a fistful of my hair, tilting my head back and kissing me. I thought we were going to continue the sexual charade when we got back to mine. I went upstairs to 'freshen up' and when I came back down to my room he was already in my bed in just his boxers.

I was drunk and didn't know what to do, I liked him so much he scared the shit out of me. I stripped down to my boring black pants and awkwardly climbed over him. I lay facing the wall in my usual position and he cuddled up to me, tucking one arm under my head and the other hand roamed free on my bare skin. I called him magic hands because his touch felt like magic. He wouldn't do anything with me, he just cuddled me to sleep even though I wanted to have sex with him. He said he didn't want to ruin our friendship with sex.

When I woke up the next morning he was wrapped around me, with his arm across my pillow. He had a tattoo down his forearm of the Led Zeppelin symbols from an old vinyl cover. I ran my finger along them and he stirred and took my hand in his. When I came back down from the shower he was sat on bed playing my guitar. I recognised the opening notes of *Wish You Were Here* by Pink Floyd.

I drove us down to work and he said goodbye to me in the car park by looping his belt around my shoulders and pulling me towards him for a hug. I turned my head to the side so there was no chance of him kissing me. I don't know why I did it.

I did it few months ago again on our daytrip to Wales. We were sat next to one another in a Weatherspoon's pub in Monmouth he stroked the side of my face and my hair but I turned away. I made sure he couldn't hold my hand whilst we were walking along by carrying my purse or jamming my hands in my pockets.

I loved him so much and he had been there for me over the few years. He had also not been there at times but in the last year he was there the most. I knew he had issues, ones that were very similar to mine. The worst part was knowing that he loved me and knowing that in those moments we had together he made me happier than anyone had ever done. He had been there when no one else had. He had always encouraged me to be the best version of me and always gave me room to mess up. I knew he would always be there but I needed more.

My friends would switch between telling me he was the one and that he loved me, to making it clear that they hated him for being a let down and not committing to me.

Danny once told me wished he had met me three years before he messed his life up and then he would have swept me off my feet. It was never clear to me why he wanted me around because he went through periods of time just being there for me and helping me achieve and refusing to sleep with me despite my advances. That wasn't good enough for me either, I just thought he didn't fancy me.

He had slept with me a lot in the last year but the Sunday after Joseph but before the Wales trip was the last time. The weekend after the trip I had reached out to him and he didn't respond and so I had to let him go. I had to move on from the constant back and forth that we had and how he could bring out the worst in me.

I missed him. I don't think I will ever find someone like him. He was like the other half of my soul but I didn't need another dysfunctional me to be with. I needed to be a functional me and have a man that worked with my insecurities and not against them.

I would always love Danny. There was no way out of that. We had been through a lot and we had pushed each other away numerous times and the last time I decided not to block him and delete his number. I would always be there for him no matter what. If I was strong enough to give Danny up then I must be strong enough to give drugs up.

Chapter Sixteen

The tall, narrow building of the pub loomed across the square. Old memories of Danny prickled my skin and anxiety etched a frown on my cold face. I wanted to turn and run but I knew I had no other options right now. The last pub I worked in was that very one I met Danny in and I was not about to turn down that path again. I could feel Xavier's presence around me and it encouraged me towards the open door. I navigated my way through the wooden top tables and metal chairs, across the bare wooden floor boards. I looked up and came face to face with a man with short, sandy hair and green eyes.

"You must be Anna!" He smiled and stuck out his hand for me to shake.

"Yeah. Sorry, what's your name?" I shook his hand and felt his warm and kind energy. He told me his name was Archie and I knew everything would be alright for now. I was in the right place and it was good to start listening to my gut instinct again. I had masked it so much and ignored it screaming at me as I went blindly headfirst into many stupid situations.

Archie showed me the basic stuff behind the bar and

down in the cellar. I was more of a practical learner and so I just wanted to get started. I was given a key fob to work the till and pretty soon a few of the regulars came in and I jumped in at the deep end.

A few hours later, my shift was almost over and the next person who was taking over from me had arrived. His name was Brad and he was quiet and a little bit geeky. His hair was a rich dark brown and black glasses framed his deep brown eyes. Brad was the same height as me and had a fit body clothed in fitted black jeans and a tight black t shirt. He looked shyly at me as he used his key fob to clock in.

"Hello, Anna. How did you first shift go?"

"I think I did alright, thanks, haven't killed anyone yet or broken anything so it's all good!"

"Well that sounds like a great start. You met Archie, then? I haven't worked any shifts with him yet but he seems really nice!"

"Yeah he's pretty cool. I think he wants me to go upstairs for a meeting when I finish at five."

"Why don't you head on up now? It's only five to five. What do you like to drink?"

"Oh no, I can't. I have to wait for my pay cheque before I can go buying drinks!"

"Don't be silly, I'll get it for you. Do you like cider?"

"Yes, Thatchers is the best! Thank you!"

"No worries. I'll have it waiting for you when you come back downstairs." He grinned at me and I noticed how perfect his teeth were and how good looking he was when he smiled. There was something special about him but for now I couldn't tell you what it was or what relevance it had to me.

Archie was sat upstairs. It seemed a lot bigger than downstairs with about ten tables of different sizes scattered around. Chairs lined around the sides of each one and one had a copper top that had been oxidised slightly so it had a green tint.

"So how do you like working here Anna?" Archie motioned for me to sit across from him.

"Well, from my first shift, it seems pretty cool. The only thing I am worried about is that I don't have any suitable clothes for work, though, and the guy who hired me said it was up to you who you were going to keep on?"

"Don't worry, how many hours are you looking for?"

"At least thirty."

"That's fine. Your contract only states eight hours but that is the same for everyone else and I won't let you down on an agreement that we make."

"Okay, that's awesome, thank you. I don't have any other commitments so I am very flexible with the days and times I can do."

"Okay, you'll be sent an email with login details for an online rota and I believe there is an app but I am old so do not know everything to do with phones." He grinned cheekily. I didn't think he was that old but then I always thought that everyone was younger than they actually were. He must have been in his thirties, late thirties. I noted his bogey coloured jumper but for some weird reason it looked okay as it made his eyes brighter.

"So is that everything, Anna? Oh no, hold on, you need money. Let me just run to the cash point. I can't give you an advance through wages as the company doesn't do that but I can give it to you out of my own pocket."

"Oh no, I couldn't. That's too much."

"No, it's fine. Wait here, I won't be long and you just pay me back when you can, okay?"

"I, thank you very much that is very kind of you," I stammered as he stood up and patted my shoulder on his way to the stairs.

I sat and looked out of the diamond leaded windows to the square. The sun was fighting against a large black cloud and the wind had picked up, taking some loose orange leaves with it. I played with the small silver necklace I had bought with me from Mum's house. My brother had given it to me at his wedding. It hung tight to my collar bones and it was a disk of silver with a family tree carved out of the middle. I had teamed it up with one of my favourite crystals that I stopped wearing when I was with Joseph. I was ready to wear it again and it looked good on the silver chain next to the family tree.

I heard footsteps coming across the wooden floor and I turned to see Archie was back.

"Here you go. And Anna, get whatever you need with it. I get the sense that you deserve it." Archie handed me a wad of cash and shook my hand again.

"Thank you. That is very kind of you, thank you so much!"

"No worries. I think Brad has the pint ready for you. Check the rota when you get home tonight for your hours! Have a good evening!" He winked and headed off to the kitchen door that split off to the office. I counted the money in my hand and outwardly gasped as he had given me two hundred pounds. The coke head in me wanted to go and spend it on drugs but I remembered how it hurt to give up Danny but I did it. This was a piece of cake. I had an alcohol downstairs and also the chance to get a wardrobe of clothes I actually wanted to wear. This time things would be different and they had to be different for me to move on in the right direction.

Chapter Seventeen

Brad was serving another guy who I had recognised from my shift earlier and I spied a free seat at the end of the bar against the wall. I could hide up in this corner and people watch.

My pint was pushed across the bar to me with a smile and I nodded in thanks. I was jaded from today's shift but I was happy. I didn't fancy going back home to an empty house and even though I knew Toad would be waiting for me I still felt lonely. I think that maybe loneliness was my trigger for bad behaviour. There was some kind of emptiness inside of me that I needed to fill. When I was around people I temporarily filled it. I didn't know how to manage my alone time just yet and I figured once I got a hold on that then my addictions and attachments to the wrong kind of people would dissipate.

I could feel Brad glancing at me every so often. I think he must have been intrigued by me and trying to work me out. The first pint buzz started to take hold and I warmed up enough for a bit of chit chat with Brad over the lager pumps. He offered me another drink when I had finished mine but I shook my head and bade him goodbye. I put my headphones back on and chose a better playlist this time. Drunk Anna loved to message Danny and even though I wasn't drunk and I hadn't messaged him for a very long time, it could go that way.

The Rolling Stones filled my ears and Keith Richards began his meandering vocals through and through to the epic drop of the many minute-ed song. I enjoyed Mick Jagger as a front man but Keith was my favourite member. He was the driving force behind the Stones and he never failed to render me speechless.

A previous boyfriend had introduced me to Keith's solo music. We used to get stoned in my car and listen to different songs. It was rare that I let someone else play music in my car but I was glad I had gotten over that stubborn pig-headedness and was able to listen to new music. When I heard *Wicked as it Seems*, I couldn't stop listening to it. I worked in London at Clapham Junction at the time and I used to listen to it five and half times from the train station to the shop front door. Some things never wore thin and then I began to wonder how I had existed this long without knowing about Keith. Apparently he had spent twenty years in Jamaica and when I watched him perform on YouTube, I could see the swagger and he was the king of the offbeat. He fascinated me and everything about him just oozed music. You could tell it was his passion and everywhere he went added more and more to his mix and soul. I couldn't stop watching the way his shoulders smoothed to the music and every beat seemed to move through him first before the rest of us were allowed to feel it.

The nights were drawing in colder and darker. The

swirling leaves scuttled across my path and I made a mental note to get a feminine, warm jumper tomorrow when I built my wardrobe back up again. I picked up my pace as I saw the house merging into view ahead.

I headed straight to Xavier's record collection and was pleased at the most of it but there was no Keith Richards. There was however some early blues. I pulled out Chuck Berry and Muddy Waters. I started off with Muddy and turned it up loud. The house was detached and I silently thanked Xavier for that. I ran up the stairs to get my laptop and threw myself on to the sofa and opened the lid. Mum's old laptop was surely made by caveman given how chunky and slow it was. I briefly wondered if that made me a caveman but quickly shook the thought from my mind. My fingers made fast work of documenting my day for a blog I had set up a long time ago. It wasn't enough for me and I needed to get my teeth into something bigger and better. The blog was cathartic and good to re-read when times were bad but I craved more. I had considered writing a book for a while but I had not had the patience or the confidence to do it. I set myself a target of fifty thousand words and that, if I managed to hit that, then I would send it off to the publishers. If I kept working at it for that amount of time then I would be able to write the whole book. I'm pretty sure I would always move the goal posts so I never had to send it to the publishers but the thought would get me started.

I decided to use my blogs and the piece of writing I had done at Mum's. I could work them into a fictional fantasy based on my life. My university tutor had told me to keep writing every day. Do not wait for creativity to come because you could be waiting an awful long time.

The click of the record finishing its first side was annoying but also welcome. I flipped the vinyl and dropped the arm onto the first track. I looked back over the three paragraphs I had printed and corrected any spelling mistakes. It was hard to read it as a book when it was on the computer screen in a word document. I grabbed a pen and paper from the kitchen and fashioned a list of things I should get tomorrow. Dresses, women's underwear and tights were a given. I wanted to get a printer and paper and also a nice woollen jumper to go over my dresses. I stopped short of a snakeskin jacket like Richards'; I didn't have the swagger that he did to pull it off.

I checked my emails and downloaded the app to my phone for the rota. I wasn't in until tomorrow afternoon so I would be able to head into town to get my wares. I checked the time and it was eight o'clock. The healing circle started at half eight and I needed to freshen up before I went down.

The church was next to the massive petrol station on Red Brick Lane that sold really cheap alcohol, lovingly called Bargain Booze. My step faltered as I approached the front door of the church. I had no idea what help I would find inside, if anything at all. Leaving my inhibitions at the door I walked in with my head high.

The room buzzed with a silent energy that I had never felt before and my necklace was almost lifting off my chest. I tried to cover it up with my hand as I didn't want to draw attention to myself but it was too late. A wizened old lady crept over to me with her eyes locked onto the silver.

She reached out a hand to touch it but I stepped back slightly. She let her hand drop and her gaze shifted to meet my own eyes. I found myself staring into the deepest pits of black that tried to pull me in and reach into my mind. I blinked to break the bond as I did not want anyone going through my messed up head.

"Anna. How lovely to meet you." She held out three crooked fingers for me to take. I quickly pumped them before grasping my necklace again. The hair on the back of my neck was on end and I felt like a cat with a bushed up tail. Every fibre in my being was screaming at me to get away from this woman, but at the same time, who was she? Besides there could be other people in this room who could help me.

"Hi, sorry I don't think we have been introduced?"

"My name is Ella!"

"Oh that's a lovely name. I must apologise but this is my first time here and I don't know what to expect or what I should do."

"Oh don't worry, little one. Just take a seat and Pat will explain everything!"

"Okay, thank you. It was lovely to meet you." I smiled briefly and then she seemed to be on roller skates, the way she glided away so quickly. This was some kind of weird, crazy dream, it had to be.

I sat as far away from her as I could at the back and was pleased to see that even though it was called a healing circle, we would be sitting in rows. I could camp out at the back until this was over.

Pat was a gentle man in his late fifties with sandy blond hair and a love of green. His whole outfit was different shades of green. Even his glasses were framed in olive. He had a calming smile and he talked us through the evening. We spent most of the time learning how to shut out other energies and centre our own. This was just as important as being able to take on other people's energy. Pat said that, in order for us to help other people, we must first learn how to care for ourselves and set clear boundaries. This was definitely something I needed to learn and as the session finished I felt like I was beginning to understand myself a little better. We were asked to stay for coffee and cake after but I could see Ella making a beeline for me again and so I thanked Pat and tried not to run out the front door.

My bed was calling me after being on my feet all day and even though I learnt about energy tonight, mine was used up now. I had worked many different professions but bar work was always the most physical. I hauled my aching legs and feet up the stairs and flopped into bed.

The next morning I woke early and ready to go. I grabbed my list and turned my nose up at the bread in the kitchen. I was becoming fast put off bread and felt like a change was needed. Now I was eating again and I needed to make sure it was the right food. I had heard horror stories of people giving up drugs and putting weight on and I definitely did not want any extra padding.

I collected what I needed from Tesco and regretted it as the printer was awkward and heavy. I ran it home and scowled at Xavier's car on my way past. I needed to somehow sort out insurance on it. The issue lay in me not being the car's legal owner, bumping the price right up. It was something for my goals list; I needed to get back behind the wheel. It had been too long.

I headed back out to complete the final part of the list and enter into unknown territory. Dress shopping had never been my forte. Actually, scrap forte, it was something I had never done despite Mum's constant efforts as I was growing up. Now was the time to embrace being a woman and to enjoy it. I will admit that most of my preference until now, was the ease of wearing boys' clothes, comfort and the fact that I could sit with my legs crossed or climb trees without flashing. The second part I think was more concerning in reference to our society. I felt that if I wore dresses or made myself look attractive, that the unwanted attention would be my fault and I would have even more men come on to me. I did not wish to have that kind of attention and I strived to be taken seriously. Now I realised that other people's behaviour was nothing to do with me or the way I dressed and I needed to stop giving other people so much power. This was my life and I needed to live it my way and stop hiding.

I walked into H&M with purpose and went straight for their dress selection. Each one I flicked past wasn't right and my shoulders sagged in defeat. Granted this was only the first shop but I wasn't a fan of shopping. I was ready to leave when I saw it. It was next to a selection of burgundy woollen jumpers and there was only one left on the rail. The slate grey dress was my size and in loose t shirt form. I tried it on right there and then over my clothes and it fit. I grabbed the burgundy jumper next to it and wriggled out of the dress. After I had grabbed some tights and a pack of black underwear. I paid at the tills and left. I had enough money left to get some more clothes and I needed shoes. Sports Direct served me well on a pair of black Converse at a discount price and I managed to find another dress whilst I was there. I checked my phone to see the time and I had an hour to go before work, so I went in early to get something to eat. It was half price after all. I opted for the chicken salad and eyed the burgers being served to the couple next to me. It was with initial jealousy but then I realised the old piglet inside of me was just wanting to rely on food as a comfort but actually it would make me feel worse.

I was stuffing the rocket and mixed leaves into my face when a text came through from Danny. My heartbeat sped up as I opened the message. My damn heart always betrayed me with him. What was I doing? I had Xavier now. Well he was somewhere else and we had never actually talked about the logistics of our relationship/ friendship. What place was I in now? Just because he was really hot and lovely does not change the fact that he lied, whether or not it was tailored to help me.

Anna, how are you? I miss you sexy xxxxx

I hated that my face had broken out into a grin and guilt was building up inside. I messaged back, I always messaged back. Once I remember reading a quote that said, 'We are all a mess and so sometimes it is best to pick your favourite mess and go with it.' No matter what I did to Danny he was still there, even when he was ignoring me for a while. I ignored him too.

I never knew what I wanted; my heart was a wayward soul. I loved so deeply but I guess at the moment I was afraid to take the jump after my last failed relationships and so I would always keep Danny around. When I got scared or my feelings hurt, I knew exactly what I was getting with Danny and so he and I could crack open a cold cider and watch the world go by, safe in our fucked up ways.

We arranged to meet after my shift later. I was due on until nine this evening and he was going to meet me at work. I had a little excitement burning in the pit of my stomach and it burnt away the guilt. I was a fool, that was exactly right.

Chapter Eighteen

The rest of my shift went quicker than expected and I was becoming a little shifty myself. Danny let me down before and part of me hoped that he would again tonight but my instincts knew he would be here soon. Sure enough, a message came through in the last hour before I clocked out, letting me know he was on his way.

Nine o'clock rolled around and I poured myself a double vodka and lemonade. It was this new vodka we had got in for the winter and it was marmalade flavoured. I sat with the regulars at the end of the bar and drank my drink too quickly. I fiddled with the straw and eyed the clock. He was slightly later than I thought and I stood up as he walked through the door. He had a slight swagger and the sharp click of his leather boots let us know he had arrived. His jeans fit well and he was wearing a black and yellow checked shirt. His beard was neatly trimmed and his dark hair styled. His lip piercing was back in place and the silver ball glinted through his beard. My ovaries groaned as I drank him in and I wiped a bit of drool from the side of my mouth.

"Anna. Looking good as always…"

"Thanks. You're not so bad yourself." I tried to smile in a flirtatious way but probably looked slightly deranged. What did this man do to me? It was ridiculous. Anytime he clicked his fingers, here I was like a puppet on his strings. He got a drink and we sat down on the comfy chairs near the men at the bar who I had been joking about with previously. Whenever Danny came over I could never believe that he was actually here and worried that he wouldn't stay long. It was so pathetic. He made me pathetic.

I shook my head to rid the self-doubt and caught him looking at me. I asked him if he wanted another drink and he asked if we could go to mine and drink there. We headed to Charlie's Shop and he got eight cans of cider. We fell in to easy step alongside one another and I stuffed my hand that was nearest him into my pocket. I didn't know if he wanted to hold my hand but I couldn't risk looking like I might be up for it. My brain reminded me that he had seen me in my best and worst states and yet he was still here. There was no reason for me to be so nervous and worried about him.

Had I completely forgotten about Xavier?

We got to my front door and I fumbled with my key in the lock. I dropped my coat and purse upstairs and he followed me. I made sure to let him know we would be sitting in the living room so we were not anywhere near the bed. I almost ran down the stairs and grabbed my laptop on the way. He sat next to me on the sofa and pulled my legs onto his lap before handing me a can of cider. I told him to put whatever he wanted on the laptop and he chose some stand-up comedy from Netflix. I downed my cider to drown out the memories of Xavier because as much as I wanted to fight it, I knew where this evening was headed. Danny was safety and I had been through the mill. He had even helped me through it sometimes.

Danny handed me another can of cider and, being the lightweight that I am, I started to float on a drunk cloud. He was so good looking while intently watching Adam Sandler on the laptop.

When it finished I told him to put something else on but the look in his eyes told me otherwise. Suddenly his lips were on mine and I wanted to resist but I couldn't. I never had been able to. I relaxed into it and my hands automatically weaved into his hair.

I blocked out all thoughts of Xavier as Danny kissed my neck and rid me of my clothes. He made love to me on the sofa and afterwards I expected him to wait a while and then leave, just like he usually did, but he insisted on staying the night. I was a little annoyed by this as I wanted to fart and hog the bed but I had waited all year for him to stay the night again.

I downed the second can of cider before wobbling up the stairs to bed and I wrapped my arm around him as he got into bed beside me. This was all wrong. He was wrong. What had I done?

If there was one thing I knew how to do well it was sabotaging my life. I had Xavier and he was so good to me. He was everything I had wanted and yet the minute he was gone. I was in bed with Danny. I silently cried myself to sleep and wished tonight to be a bad dream but somewhere and somehow, I could feel Xavier telling me everything was going to be okay. I didn't feel like I deserved it but hopefully the light of day would bring me promise.

I woke to Danny getting his clothes on and he kissed me goodbye. It was still dark and he had work early. As soon as I heard the front door close behind him, I lifted my leg and let out a long fart. I knew I farted in the night but I had to not care. He still came back time and time again. My head pounded gently with the dregs of cider from last night as I sat up. My mouth tasted like an old piece of rubber so I decided it best for me to sleep in a little longer.

Chapter Nineteen

The sun blared through the open windows and I winced as I opened my eyes. I had a few seconds left of pure hangover and no memories of the night before. Then it came flooding in and sick rose up in my throat. I ran to the bathroom and emptied my stomach into the toilet. I thought I was done with this, I thought I was over the self sabotage but I had just had sex with another man in Xavier's house. Not to mention drinking. Why couldn't I leave it alone? I had been given the chance to move on and start again and I had just fucked it up. I knew what I had to do and I had to do it sooner rather than later. I just hoped that it would work.

I shuffled down the garden after having a long and hot shower. My hair was soaking into the fabric of Xavier's hoodie. Maybe I hoped to look more vulnerable in his clothes but I knew he would be done with me now. That meant I was out on the street with nothing and the thought of cocaine was ringing in my pounding head.

I made it to the mirror and drew a long breath before looking up. My reflection stared back and there was no magic this time. It was just disappointing old me with wet ratty hair and a pale face. I called out to Xavier but nothing happened. A tear escaped and ran down my face. No matter what I did or how many times I called his name, nothing happened. I grabbed the mirror and cried into it, desperate to see his beautiful face and to hear him tell me it would be okay.

I messed up the only thing that made sense and the only thing that made me think twice about constantly fucking my life up.

The mirror shattered as I smashed my fist into it. Shards of glass embedded into my knuckles. I sank to the floor and cried big fat noisy tears. I had lost him. I had lost him because I was too selfish to change, too selfish to face my demons.

Toad zoomed down the garden and ran circles round my head. I felt a little better with him there and I knew he was trying to send me loving energy. He kept on and finally he settled on my shoulder. It warmed me enough to make me stand up and pick the bits of mirror out of my hand. It was already swollen and very bloody. I stumbled up to the back door and over to the sink in the kitchen. Blood swirled down the drain and I winced in pain as the cold water ran over my bruised and broken skin. Even though Toad was still sat lovingly on my shoulder, silent tears flowed down my face as I realised that I had destroyed my only way of contacting Xavier because I had let my emotions take over. I wished that I could rewind the past twenty-four hours and stop myself from ruining all that was good in my life.

Toad buzzed gently on my shoulder before flying over to the cupboard and making a scene, whizzing up and down in front of it. I wrapped my now clean hand in a tea towel and opened the cupboard door. Inside it was full of medical supplies. I wrapped my hand up as best I could and retired to the sofa. I needed to talk to Archie and let him know what I had done to my hand. Could I get sacked for this? I started to panic. I was still in my probation period and my job was currently the only thing I had left.

Archie answered after the first ring.

"Archie, it's Anna."

"I know. How are you? How are you finding work so far?"

"Good thanks. Listen are you around later today for a short meeting?"

"Yeah but only within the next half an hour if you can make it down? I am back to back with meetings this afternoon!"

"I'll come down now, and thank you." I hung up and grabbed my headphones and the bag of cider cans, some empty and some full. I hurled all of them into the outside bin and stomped down to work.

Brad was on the bar when I pushed the front door of the pub open. There were a few people in and a couple of regulars. I tried to conceal my injury behind my back but Brad had already seen it. He pulled me aside as I went to the bottom of the stairs. "Anna, what happened to you?"

"I'm fine I just had an accident. I'm fine."

"Are you sure? Is someone taking care of you? What about that guy from last night?"

"Yeah it's fine, he was just a friend. Sorry but I have to go and meet Archie." I cringed as I pushed past him and clambered up the stairs.

Archie was already up there tidying behind the bar.

"Anna, how are you? Sorry I'm cleaning up after this last manager; the place is a mess!"

I could see the bags under his eyes as he put down the box on the bar top. I felt even worse as I knew I would be loading even more work on to his already burdened shoulders. Tears spilled down my face for the second time today and I bowed my head in shame.

"Anna, what did you do to you hand and why are you crying? Did someone hurt you?"

"No, it was just me and my stupidity. Now I'm going to lose this job and it's all I have."

"No, you're not. Anna, for some reason I have faith in you and I know that whatever happened you do not need any more stress on your shoulders. You have shown you are a good worker in your first couple of shifts and I can tell you have come from somewhere rough."

"It's all my fault!" I sobbed, clutching my hand close to my chest.

"I want you to take some time off okay? You need to promise me you will get to the doctor's right away. I can sort you a week's holiday and that's all I can manage."

"How can you give me holiday? I haven't earnt it!"

"I can sort it for you. It's necessary to keep you as a worker and you need your hands to work."

"I don't deserve this."

"Maybe what you need to do is stop thinking you don't deserve the good things that happen and accept that you are human. Go to the doctor's and come back to work in a week. Let me know what the doctor say, please."

"Thank you." I scuttled off down the stairs and out the back door. I knew I had no hope with the doctor but I could go to the walk-in centre.

I sat for what seemed like an age in the waiting room. I had this horrible feeling that I was being watched as I flicked through social media on my phone. I switched my phone on to locked mode and used the screen as a mirror to see behind me. I gasped and almost dropped my phone as two pits of black shone and then disappeared. The triage nurse finally called my name and I almost ran to her office. She assessed the damage and felt that underneath the cuts it was just sprained. She wrapped it up properly for me and told me to keep it clean and come back again if it didn't look any better in a few days. Her main concern was the broken skin from the mirror shards but I had somehow managed to get it all out and she was satisfied that it would heal without stitches.

I felt stupid as I walked across the square and home. As I approached the front door, Toad zoomed down past the car and ran circles round my head.

"Hey Toad. Have you been guarding the house for me?"

He purred next to my ear in response and zoomed back to the front door. I could feel he was excited about something and I just wanted to crawl in to bed and cry. I knew I should make myself eat something and toast seemed like the best option. As I was waiting for it to pop up, Toad kept bumping against the back door.

"You want me to go outside?" I asked him. He buzzed round and round my head before going back to the door. I abandoned my toast and wandered out, down the gardening. I expected Toad wanted me to clean the broken mirror up. To be honest it was awful of me to have left it out there. I had briefly seen the next door neighbour's cat wandering around and it could have cut its feet on the broken shards.

When I got to the mirror it was whole again and there was just no blood on it. How on earth was it whole again? There was no mess on the grass. It was like it had not happened at all. A shadow appeared in the mirror.

"Do you want him back?" The shadow asked. It had a growling voice and it made my skin prickle.

"I would do anything to get him back."

"Anything?"

"You heard what I said!" I levelled a hard stare back into the mirror. The shadow laughed and my world went black.

Chapter Twenty

Sunlight. Sunlight was searing through the blackness and my hand was pulsing with energy. I was in the garden and everything looked the same. Everything was just as it was before. I was laid out on the cold grass a little way from the mirror. My dress was only slightly damp on the backside and I was still in Xavier's hoodie. I sat up and the energy was still buzzing in my hand. I looked at it and the bandage slowly fell away to reveal a golden light humming around my wound. Less than a minute later, the buzzing stopped and I carefully inspected my injured hand. Though it was now no longer damaged and the skin was fresh and clean with no scarring.

I studied my surrounds in more detail and noticed the dahlias were the same but usually they would be starting to deteriorate this long into their flowering cycle. I got to my feet and went right up to the large-headed flowers. They were stunning and each of the many petals were perfect. There was not a mark on any of them and they were as full as if the flowers had only just burst.

I shrugged my shoulders and ambled up the garden to the back door. My toast was waiting, popped and ready in the toaster. I pushed the slices back down for a reheat and leant against the counter. I suddenly remembered the tomato soup in the cupboard and so I put it in the microwave for two minutes.

Later on that evening I went up to the Stone Age laptop and wrote some more of my story. My mistakes were only mistakes if I didn't learn from them and typing was a lot easier without a bandage around my hand. It helped to write out my night with Danny. I wasn't a bad person and, coming from a bad place, I still had demons that were misplaced and floated around, trying to find a new slot to fit in. If I was to move on then I needed to have like-minded people around me. I wasn't fucked in the head, I just let myself believe in that so I might fit in and accept people's bad behaviour. Writing seemed to be my saviour. You know what, no. I was my saviour. With that epiphany I went to bed and had a long sleep.

The next morning I stood in my new favourite spot in the kitchen. There wasn't a cloud in the sky and it was beautiful. There also wasn't a Toad in the sky... I whistled and called him but he never came. How odd. He must have an important job to do and I probably shouldn't interrupt him. Still, it was rude that he hadn't asked me first before he disappeared.

I went out to the garden and searched. The mirror was the same and so were the dahlias. I made myself some breakfast and got ready for work.

I tucked my necklace into my jumper as I walked down the road and I jammed my headphones on. I was distracted, trying to choose a song from my many millions of carefully created playlists I had on my phone. I fancied some liquid drum and bass and my feet bounced along the pavement as I slid my phone back into my pocket. I shut my eyes for a second to bathe in the sun and when I opened them again I could see a car driving too close to me. They slowed as they drove past and I jumped when I saw the black eyes of the driver staring at me. I shook my head in disbelief and tried to focus on the music.

A man came towards me walking a little white dog. The dog's eyes were black. I looked up to the man's face and his eyes were black. I took off at a faster pace to work and kept my head down making damn sure that I didn't look at anyone else on the way there but I knew all of their eyes would be black as well.

I flew in the door to work and shut it carefully behind me, pleased to be safe and even more pleased when I heard Archie call my name and good morning. My shoulders sagged with relief and I turned to look at him, all the time wondering how I could explain the people's eyes and how my hand was healed.

My stomach plummeted as I looked into the place where his green eyes would usually glitter but black stared back.